FLAMBARDS

Also by K. M. Peyton

FLAMBARDS DIVIDED

DEAR FRED

GOING HOME

FLAMBARDS

K. M. Peyton

Illustrated by Victor G. Ambrus

PHILOMEL BOOKS
New York

To Bernadette and Catherine

Library of Congress Cataloging in Publication Data
Peyton, K. M.   Flambards.
Reprint. Originally published: London:
Oxford University Press, c1967.
Summary: A twelve-year-old orphan girl is faced
with a radically different way of life when she is
sent to live with a crippled, tyrannical uncle who
is obsessed with hounds and horses and who expects
her and his two sons to follow in his footsteps.
[1. Orphans–Fiction.   2. Horsemanship–Fiction.
3. England–Fiction]   I. Ambrus, Victor G., ill.   II. Title.
PZ7.P4483Fl   1982   [Fic]   82-22391
ISBN 0-399-20925-5

Contents

PART ONE: *1908*

A Hunting Accident

The fox was running easily. He came up the hill through the short wet grass, dropped into a ditch, and ran up through the flowing water. The ditch was deep, overgrown with hawthorn, and overhung with enormous elms whose last yellow leaves were gleaming against the sky: a wet November sky, heavy over the hill and over the brimming, water-streaked valley below.

A man cutting the hedge saw the fox break cover a hundred yards along and streak away over the adjoining pasture. For a moment it was silhouetted on the crest of the hill, a big dog fox that had played the game before. The man sniffed, and rested his pruning tool. In his leather jacket and muddy breeches he was invisible in the shadow of the hedge. He would watch and say nothing. "They'll get no help from me," he was thinking. "Or as much as I get from them, which is the same thing. See all, say nowt." The thought gave him a nice satisfaction, to break the monotony of slaving from dawn till dark.

Hounds were not long appearing. They poured through the hedge in the lower pasture and came up the hill all in a bunch, making a noise which stirred the stomach of the man, for all his sour thoughts. Even the huntsman was not up with them, and the field was strung out across half a mile of grazing below. The pack of hounds tumbled and scrambled into the hawthorn and broke up momentarily, some bursting out into the far field, some casting along the hawthorn roots. Swirling, yelping, the smooth wave checked, like water dividing among rocks; then an excited tongue from down the ditch drew it together again. The lost, bounding novices wheeled to follow, launching themselves frantically back into the muddy ditch: a splashing, a cracking of branches, a shower of dying leaves like gold pennies and hounds were away, tumbling out into the open with the scent high in their nostrils.

As their clamor died away, the man was conscious of the respite, hearing them go, waiting for what he knew was coming. He shrank back, brown against the brown elm trunks. The air stank of rotting leaves, the musk of the fox. He had seen it before, the farmworker, and knew how his own common sense became overruled. Already the thud of hoofs was in his boot soles. He braced himself, his knuckles tight on the pruning tool, and watched the spots of red burst out of the trees below. Check, wheel: he could see the score marks of iron-shod hoofs in the wet grass, then the pounding in the hillside like its own heart beating and the first breast of a big bay horse in his vision, its breath roaring, the huntsman shouting his encouragement as he viewed hounds on the far slope. The man was glancing around for a way through. There was a gate at the far end, but a wasting of precious ground to go through it; the worker knew the man would jump, and there was only one possibility: a slight gap in the hawthorn and the ditch deep and ugly below, the approach uphill.

The huntsman went through, holding his arm up as the bare twigs thrust at him. The phalanx of riders behind, pounding up the hill, snarled up, separating, some making for the gate, some for the gap, and cursing anyone in their way. The ground shook to the uphill gallop of lathered, shining horses,

foam on their bits, eyes frenzied with excitement. Only the
thrusters, the ones riding close to the hounds, made for the
gap: there was a shouting of advice, some doubt, and a horse
pulled up in a great flurry of mud for a sudden failing of courage on the part of his rider. The horse behind was crossed and
its rider swore. He was just a boy, but his swearing, and the
fury in his eyes, were those of a man. He gave his balked
horse a crack with his whip and went for the gap at an angle,
when any sane man would have gone back for a fresh approach.
The horse made a desperate leap and in mid-air its rider was
twisting around, shouting behind him: "Come on, Will! It's
all right!" There were only three horses to follow, most of the
field having opted for the gate, and of these the leader was a
gray, whose rider was also a boy, even younger than the one
in front. The gray, its nostrils red with blood, its eyes wild
with excitement, pounded toward the gap and the tail of its
stablemate, and the boy on top hadn't the strength to change
its course. That he wanted to was evident. Unlike the boy in
front, his face was closed with fear. Sweat and mud streaked
a greenish pallor. His dark eyes, seeing the hedge loom, flared
with terror. He flung himself forward, his fingers twisting in
the horse's mane, reins flying, but the horse jumped even bigger than the boy was expecting. His seat, the grip of his thin
legs, were not enough to hold the boldness of the big, peppered
gray gelding; the twigs whipped the boy's face and he fell backward and sideways through the cracking branches and heavily
into the bottom of the ditch. The gray scarcely felt its loss,
landed in a smother of flying mud, and galloped on.

"'Ware young Will!"

The man behind dragged at his horse and pulled it from the
lip of the ditch to a scorching halt. The other rider also pulled
up cursing, and the worker slipped out of the cover of the
elms and was first in the ditch beside the boy, while the other
men were still tangled up with their wheeling horses.

"Is he bad?"

The men were hoping they could ride on, but the worker
said, "Yes, sir. He's bad all right."

"Ah, damn the brat!" one of the men muttered under his breath. Then, resignedly, "I'll ride down to the Hall, Tom. Tell 'em what's happened. You'll stay with him, eh?"

"Yes, I'll stay."

A few tailenders cantered up to see what was amiss, and between them they dragged the boy out of the ditch and on-to the grass. He was barely conscious, but screamed when he was moved, and the men shook their heads.

"That's bad, eh?"

"Who is it?"

"Young Russell, from Flambards."

"Oh, aye, young William. My God, what'll the old man say about it?"

"He'd worry more if it were Mark."

"This were Mark's fault, I'd say," remarked the man who had seen the fall. "Will was following his brother. Mark went through, like the madcap he is, and shouted Will to follow. Never thought to tell him the gate. Shrimp like Will, to try a place like that!"

"Couldn't stop, I reckon. No more strength than a girl. Not like young Mark."

"That Mark! He's a real chip off the old block. Old Russell all over again."

"He never thought to come back, didn't Mark . . ."

Somebody rode off to fetch a sheepfold gate, and the others stood around dutifully, having done their best for the boy: laid him in the grass, straightened out his broken limbs, and loosened his collar. He was a thin, fine-featured boy, small for his thirteen years. His long fingers were still clenched with trying to steady the big gray, the palms of his hands raw. The horses stood, steaming, snatching at their bits, circling impatiently with a creak of saddle leather and squelch of hoofs. The hounds had long gone and the rooks were coming back to the elms, circling and croaking.

The sheepfold gate was fetched and William Russell was laid on it and carried off, lurching, down the hill by four of the hunting men. Two of them led their own horses, and the farmworker followed with the two others, thinking, "This'll be sixpenceworth, for sure, a shilling with luck. Well done, young Will, you chose your spot nicely."

Five miles away hounds lost the scent in a field of sheep. Mark Russell pulled up and looked behind him for the first time since the jump out of the Hall meadows, and was surprised to see Woodpigeon, William's gray, coming loose, reins and stirrups flying. He rode his own horse off to head him, shouting at him in his rough, imperious voice:

"You old fool horse! Woodpigeon, steady on!" The big gray

pulled up and Mark caught his reins, glancing him over for
damage.

"And what have you done with that nincompoop Will?
Killed him, you old fool horse?"

Christina Parsons sat upright in the pony cart, watching the
sodden autumn fields trot past, hoping it would not rain before they reached Flambards, and spoil her new hat. The
groom who sat beside her had apologized for the pony cart,
explaining that the carriage had had to go out unexpectedly,
and if he had waited for it to come back he would have missed
meeting her train. Since the explanation he had, respectfully,
ventured no more. Christina, not quite sure if a lady traveling
alone spoke to grooms, decided not to risk it and stared at the
countryside in silence. She looked very self-possessed, perhaps
more so than she felt, for in her twelve years she had come to
the conclusion that it was rash to show one's feelings too
quickly; life had already dealt her some cruel surprises, and the
present surprise had yet to reveal its nature, cruel or otherwise.

"Uncle Russell wants you to go and live at Flambards,"
Aunt Grace had said, in some astonishment, over the breakfast
table. "Well!" And then, "Well!" again, this time with a hint
of indignation.

Christina had heard of Flambards, and Uncle Russell, but
had not seen or met either. Nor terribly wanted to, from what
she had heard.

"Live with him? What's wrong with things the way they
are?"

She had been beginning to get used to Aunt Grace, after a
year. She was a lot better than Aunt Mildred, the one before,
and second-cousin Jessica before that. As an orphan since the
age of five, Christina had become used to being shuttled around
between the various female relatives in the suburbs of London.
But Uncle Russell at Flambards, forty miles out in the country
. . . this was a new departure altogether. Uncle Russell had
never so much as inquired after her before.

"Why does he bother now?" as Aunt Grace quickly put it,
her voice full of suspicion.

"He's after the money," Christina said, having heard it so often before. She knew, not because anyone had ever told her so but because she had become adept at listening to grown-up conversations when everyone thought she was concentrating on her sewing or her reading, that her parents had left her a lot of money. When she was twenty-one, she would be rich. It was a comfortable thought, but remote, and nothing to do with her present situation. But the adults talked about it a lot. Christina was vague about her relations, but when she thought hard about it she remembered that Uncle Russell was her dead mother's half-brother. Her mother had married a rich young man called Julian Parsons, and they had died together when a packet boat had foundered in the English Channel six years ago. Uncle Russell, Christina remembered hearing, had said, "Serve 'em right for being so damned rich."

"I thought Uncle Russell was rich, though?" Christina said, wanting to get things straight.

"Was rich, dear. Emphasize the was. Yes." Aunt Grace was stirring her tea absently. Aunt Grace, once a Russell, now the widow of a bank clerk, made a fair living for herself as a dressmaker. She did not mind having Christina to live with her, but found her an embarrassment at times, as she lived in hopes of even yet attracting another husband.

"What happened to Uncle Russell's money?" Christina asked.

"Flambards took it, and the life he lived, like his father before him. All this hunting—the horses he bought, and the hounds! All he thought about. Still does, I believe, in spite of his accident. He gave up the hounds, but the stables are still full of horses, from what I hear. And only the two boys to ride them. Uncle Russell can scarcely get out of his chair these days."

Christina did not think the prospect very attractive. Her life so far had been spent entirely with the female sex, and Flambards seemed to be exclusively male. And she had no great love of horses.

"Who looks after the house, then?"

"Since Isabel died—your Uncle Russell's wife—there's nobody save the servants. And the Lord only knows, Russell's so difficult, he's got them all in tears and giving in their notice before the first week's out." Aunt Grace checked herself, realizing she was not giving Christina much encouragement. "But there, you'll have two young cousins to play with. It's time you saw somebody your own age."

Christina wished they were girls. But she did not argue; she was used to being moved about, following an exchange of letters, or a family discussion. It never occurred to anybody that she should ever be consulted as to what was best for her. It never occurred to Christina, either, that she should. Being told so little, she had learned to use her wits to find out more of what she wanted to know. She was not above a little eavesdropping, or peeking at letters, when her future was in doubt, and the most interesting snippet of information concerning Uncle Russell's sudden interest in her came to her in this way. Aunt Grace had had to answer the door in the middle of writing a letter, and Christina, pretending (even to herself) that she wanted to adjust the gas, got up from her sewing and crossed over to the hissing gas fixture over Aunt Grace's bureau. The wet ink gleamed on the paper: ". . . shall miss her. Of course, the next thing we shall hear, if I know my dear half-brother, is that she will be married to Mark, and Flambards will be back on its feet again for another few years. I am sure that is what lies behind it. How else, save through an advantageous marriage, will the poor place be propped up much longer? Russell is—"

Christina's eyes opened very wide. She leaped back to her sewing and went on with her hemming rather recklessly, making stitches that Aunt Grace was later to rip out, with much tut-tutting.

Christina had never been in the country much before—not country where there was no comforting acreage of stucco and cobbles within easy walking distance. She was used to riding behind the bus-horses, or in a hansom, but not in an open trap, and was amazed at the miles of fields and woods they passed through, with no houses in sight. Under the gray sky she thought it a rather depressing sight, the dark lacework of the naked elms making a stark pattern over her head, the grass strips splashed with mud and the ditches swollen. The road was narrow and rough, and they met only two other carts, and two riders in scarlet jackets to whom the groom beside Christina touched his cap. The men were covered in mud and their horses in sweat. Christina knew that they had been hunting and, seeing them, she was very conscious of her new life starting. It came to her coldly and suddenly—that this was real. The first cold drops of rain stung her face; the afternoon was already turning dark. The sodden woods stood thick and silent. A great shiver of self-pity shook her, and she had to steel herself not to cry, clasping her hands under the rug the groom had tucked around her. Similar situations in the past had taught her how to cope. With iron self-will she switched her mind to designing herself a new dress, shutting her eyes and summoning a vision of lavender taffeta, threaded with silver ribbons. Her visions on these occasions were never bounded by the practical considerations Aunt Grace had always brought to bear on making her clothes; she concentrated on extravagance, dining at the Palace, dancing into the small hours all lace and décolleté.

"This is Flambards, miss."

Christina opened her eyes again, and found that the trap was turning left through a pair of gates. A long drive stretched ahead, bounded on the right by a wood and on the left by grazing railed off with an iron fence. At the top of the drive stood the house, but it was so covered with ivy that from a distance Christina could make no guesses as to the architecture that lay beneath. The horse's hoofs spat up gravel. Christina, with signs of civilization in sight, felt optimistic and nervous all together, but no longer like crying.

The house, on closer examination, was a mid-Victorian pile with large bay windows. The drive ran up to the front door. To the right a rambling garden spilled onto the gravel edge, a garden of overgrown roses—some still flowering, balled with wet like tight pink cabbages—and long grass, with a fine cedar tree set in the middle of what had once been the lawn. On the left the drive passed the house and curved away behind it toward a tangle of walls and tiled roofs beyond, which Christina supposed was the stables. Some big chestnut trees, now gaunt frames of black, downspreading branches, lined the drive as it curved away; great heaps of rotted leaves lay tumbled below, with burst horse chestnuts spat out over the gravel, the shells shriveled like little brown oranges. The groom stopped the horse in front of the door, and helped Christina down from the cart. Nobody seemed to be waiting for her.

"I'll carry your trunk into the hall, miss. Go in. The door will be open."

"Thank you."

Christina crossed into the porch, which was full of muddy boots, and nervously pushed open the door. She found herself in a big cold hall, with an old foxhound pushing at her skirts. A thin, worn-looking woman, obviously a servant, was coming through a doorway on one side to greet her, and in a doorway on the other side a man on crutches appeared with a bound that gave Christina a start.

"Is it William?" he said. Seeing Christina, he added, "Oh, no. It's you."

"It's Miss Christina, sir," said the woman.

"Yes, well—see to her," the man said shortly; very rudely, Christina thought, lifting her chin.

She looked at him, having heard so much of Uncle Russell, and found him not unlike what she had imagined: a big but shrunken-looking man, with heavy shoulders overdeveloped by the crutches, and spindly, trailing legs. He had a craggy red face ("Drink," Christina said to herself knowingly), a flattened broken nose, and very fierce eyes. She thought immediately, "I shall keep out of his way," feeling that, with those legs, he would be easily eluded. She said politely, "How do you do, Uncle," but he took no notice.

"Tell me when William comes," Russell said to the woman, but the groom, coming in with Christina's trunk, said, "The carriage is coming up the drive now, sir, and Dr. Porter right behind."

Through the open door the scrunch of several lots of hoofs could be heard on the gravel. The woman said quickly to Christina, "I'll see to you in a minute, miss. Everything's happening at once. Master William's had an accident."

Christina shrank back out of the way as everyone went to the door. She was not at all sorry to have her arrival overshadowed in this way, being used to taking a place in the background of every house she could remember. In a strange way it made her feel at home. The fact that Master William had had an accident did not come as a surprise either, after Aunt Grace's descriptions of the hazards of the hunting field. She felt no compassion, only a morbid curiosity to see what had happened to him. She hoped there were no bones sticking out. "At least it isn't Mark," she thought, for she was very interested in finding out what Mark looked like.

William was carried into the hall on the sheepfold gate. Christina, peering, saw a pathetic bundle of mud-stained hunting clothes and a white, upturned face, scratched with blood. To her surprise, she was instantly moved with pity. He looked so small and crushed, and so frail; she had pictured a strapping youth bravely biting his lips and smiling through his pain, but not this utterly vanquished child whose face showed only fear and bewilderment.

Uncle Russell swung across to look at him as the men paused at the foot of the stairs. He looked angry and stared at William with what Christina thought was contempt (or was it merely his natural expression?). He said nothing to him, but barked at the doctor, "Well?"

"Smashed patella, certainly. Femur possibly. I'll tell you more when I've examined him."

"Horse all right?" Russell said to the groom.

"As far as we know, sir. He didn't stop."

"Woodpigeon wouldn't," Russell said. It seemed to give him satisfaction. "All right. Take him up. That'll finish his hunting for the season. Someone gone to fetch Woodpigeon?"

"Yes, sir. Dick's gone."

"Good."

The awkward burden was manhandled up the stairs, and the thin-faced servant followed it. She turned and said to Christina, "Come along. I'll show you your room. But then I'll have to wait on the doctor. We've no more help here."

Christina hurried after her. "Perhaps, if you like, there's something I could do."

"It's no task for a girl," the woman said. "But I might be glad of your help afterwards. Later on." She turned and looked at Christina, taking her in more closely than before. Then, Christina had been another body to clear up after, and feed; now, with the girl's remark, the woman saw that she might be more use than trouble.

"You must understand, dear, we're very rough in this house." She spoke softly and quickly, as if to an ally. "There's only me and Violet to do it all; I do my best, but I'm only one person. Violet lives out. When something like this happens, his lordship down there—" she jerked her head downstairs to the door where Russell had disappeared— "expects us all to get on as usual. He won't get a nurse. Of course, if it was a horse, that would be different. . . ."

"Mary!" It was the doctor bawling from the landing.

"Coming, sir!"

The woman pointed on down the corridor. "That's your room. Last door on the left."

They stood on one side to let the men who had carried the gate go back down the stairs, then Mary scurried into the room where the doctor was waiting, and the door closed behind her. Christina looked at the door, and gave a small sigh of sympathy for the boy, her cousin. Like her, he was obviously not used to being mothered. There were times, Christina knew, when it would be very nice to feel loved and wanted and pampered, and she felt that this was one of the times, for William. "But he must be used to it," she thought, remembering Russell's contemptuous face. "Like me." She felt a pang for William, and a faint, exciting optimism: he might turn out to be a good friend. She had not been expecting too much of her cousins up to now, as far as making friends was concerned. She was expecting to be snubbed and humiliated, in the way that most girls seemed to be treated by boys, in her experience. But William, for some weeks at least, would be in no position to humiliate her. "Poor William," Christina thought, genuinely moved by his plight. She had no idea what either a patella or a femur was, but knew that anything broken was exceedingly painful.

In being sorry for William, she had no time for being sorry for herself. True, her welcome had hardly been warm, but the servant—housekeeper, she must be, Christina thought—showed signs of being an ally. Uncle Russell was no more nor less than she had been led to believe. Mark had yet to be revealed. Christina walked down the corridor and opened the door of the last room on the left, and immediately marked up another notch on the credit side of her new home: the room was charming, much bigger and prettier than any she had ever been given before.

On closer inspection, it was shabby. The wallpaper, a close design of pink and brown flowers, like old-fashioned muslin, was faded, the washstand china was chipped, and the patchwork quilt was all coming apart, but the general effect was pretty and homely, with a big window looking out over the garden, and the ivy trailers creeping around the panes. There was plenty of furniture, a big wardrobe, a dressing table, and a chest beside the brass bed and marble-topped washstand, and a carpet on the floor which, after Aunt Grace's cold linoleum, Christina looked at with great satisfaction. Her trunk stood at the foot of the bed. She opened it and started to put her things away, leaving out her navy-blue serge as a suitable dress to change into for dinner. Christina was used to taking care of herself.

At twelve, Christina was a slightly plump girl, with the beginnings of a bust (which she rather resented), a fine creamy skin, and an upright carriage forced on her by the naggings of her female relatives. Her expression was guarded, her features more accustomed to showing obedience than animation. But her dark blue eyes were honest, her mouth composed, and she had a head of thick brown hair which Aunt Grace had once said was a gift straight from heaven. It fell down to her waist, curling just enough to spare Christina the arduous task of putting in curlers, but not enough to be too painful to comb. She combed it now, standing before the window, and wondered what she should do when she was finished. She did not fancy going down to Uncle Russell. She took as long as she could about washing and changing, and became painfully aware that she was very hungry indeed. No sounds came from the room across the corridor, and Mary was nowhere to be seen.

"She might be there all night," Christina thought. "And I can't sit here that long."

She had no alternative but to go downstairs. "I'll go and find myself some tea," she decided.

With a watchful eye below on what she thought of as Uncle Russell's lair, Christina descended the stairs. The stair carpet was threadbare, she noticed, and the foxhound had been joined by a second, grizzled with age. They sat by the front door and slowly thumped their tails at the sight of her.

"Not tails," Christina remembered, "but sterns. Like boats." Aunt Grace had always corrected her, with a small sigh of pain, even after all these years of not hunting any more. "Hounds wave their sterns, dear, not wag their tails." Christina had always been more interested in trying to picture Aunt Grace on a horse. She skirted the hounds cautiously, never having cared much for dogs—especially smelly ones.

She crossed to the door which Mary had come out of earlier —assuming it led to the kitchen—but became aware at the same time of hoofs once more scrunching on the gravel outside the door. The foxhounds got up, their old eyes brightening; Christina heard voices outside, and felt a hot flush of panic spread through her. She slipped through the door, shut it quickly behind her, and stood in blessed solitude in a dim, flagged passage. Having acted on impulse, she realized at once that she had behaved in an unladylike fashion. She should have waited to meet whoever it was, instead of skulking around the backstairs like a burglar. But now it was too late—and she was glad.

"Mary!" The newcomer's voice was that of a boy's, recently broken. Mark, Christina guessed. Eavesdropping, she heard the thud of Uncle Russell's crutches across the hall.

"Oh, there you are. Mary's busy with William. God knows when we'll get any dinner. Had a good day?"

"Yes! Found in Brick Kilns and killed in Wood End. Not bad, eh? Then we drew Burley Wood and put up a brace, ran to Chancellor's, and lost him in a drain."

"How did Treasure go, then? Suit you?"

"He goes all right. Can't stop him, in fact. Jumps as big as Woodpigeon, and faster. Is Will home?"

"Yes. Did you see what happened?"

"No. He was following me all right, next I saw was Woodpigeon all on his own. He didn't fall, so I don't know why Will had to come off."

"Well, he won't have the chance again for a while. His leg is smashed."

"Oh. Is Mary up there now?"

"Yes, with Porter."

"What about dinner, then?"

"Hmm. Violet's gone home. Wait, though, we've got another girl in the house now. Hetty's girl has come—what's her name? She ought to be able to cook. What's her name, d'you remember?"

"Oh, you mean from Aunt Grace? Annabel, or something? Christabel?"

To Christina's horror, Uncle Russell dragged himself to the foot of the stairs and bawled, "Christabel!"

Christina swallowed nervously. Years of embarrassment in strange houses gave her a stiffening of courage: to be out of place was nothing new, but all the same she felt herself going pink with confusion as she opened the door and emerged behind the two men.

"Did you call me?"

Uncle Russell turned around from the foot of the stairs in surprise. "Oh, there you are. I thought you were upstairs." The old man stared at her more closely than at their introduction. Christina met his gaze uncomfortably, very much aware of Mark out of the corner of her eye but not daring to take her attention from her uncle.

"Look here, you might as well make yourself at home," Russell was saying. "You'll have to find your way about sooner or later. Go and see what Mary's got in the pantry, and get some food on the table. Mark, go and show her where the things are. And get a move on. We're all famished."

Mark crossed the hall and came to the door beside her. He looked rather annoyed. Christina had a good look at him, her curiosity overcoming shyness, but in the dusk she could not see his features clearly. He was tall, black-haired, wearing a scarlet jacket covered with mud; he gave the impression of great vitality, although he was obviously tired. He contrasted strangely with the crippled hulk of his father, whose vitality lived only in the bitter, black eyes. Christina could still feel the black eyes on her after she had retreated through the door and was following Mark down the corridor.

"I'd forgotten you were coming," Mark was saying quite amiably now. "Sorry you had to arrive when the place is up-side-down. Although it's usually a bit of a mess here," he added. "Not like when Mother was around. God, I'm hungry."

"Yes, so am I," Christina said feelingly.

They were in the kitchen, looking around with a fellow eagerness for signs of food. The kitchen was large, lit with kerosene lamps, and the big wooden table in the middle was littered with half-prepared vegetables. A smell of burning meat was coming from the range, and Christina picked up a cloth and opened the oven door. A leg of mutton, slightly shriveled but awash in rich fat, tickled her nose invitingly.

"Well, that's something," Mark said. "Heave it out. We can eat it with bread. I'm not waiting for potatoes."

Apart from giving orders, he did not seem to be intending

to help, for he went into a dark scullery and started to wash. Christina, appalled at the task before her and frightened of Uncle Russell's reaction if it was not to his liking, had to take a long, cool look around to stop the panic rising again. Almost as if Aunt Grace stood beside her, she could hear the firm voice: "Be sensible, child. You are perfectly capable." Aunt Grace, no doubt, would still know her way around this gloomy kitchen. But Christina felt like crying.

She bit her lip hard. "There must be a pantry," she thought desperately, and saw one at once. She picked a lamp off the table and started to investigate. By the time Mark came out of the scullery, she had found bread and butter and a cold apple pie and put them on the table, together with some plates which were warming in the oven.

"Good," said Mark.

The lamp cast dark shadows on his face. For a boy, it was already a strong face, the eyes very direct, almost black like his father's. The hunting clothes, white stock and red jacket, suited him to perfection; unfamiliar to Christina, the clothes emphasized the strangeness of this new place. This desperation, born of weariness, uncertainty and hunger, shook her again, and she said, her voice shaking slightly, "Where do we eat it then? Where shall I lay the table?"

"In the dining room, of course," Mark said rather impatiently. He picked up the pie. "I'll show you."

The dining room, Christina discovered, was what she called Uncle Russell's lair. It was a long room, with a fire burning at one end, where Uncle Russell sat crouched in a leather chair. The walls on either side of the fireplace were lined with books. The dining table was enormous, a vast shining acreage of mahogany on which Mark set the apple pie rather incongruously.

"The knives and forks . . ." He nodded toward the sideboard which filled one wall. He then crossed to the fire and stood with his back to it, and started to tell his father about the day's sport.

Christina, with hot cheeks, pulled open the drawers of the

sideboard. There was no cloth to be found, so she set the cutlery on the bare table and went back to the kitchen. Several
journeys, the last one with the hot, shriveled meat, saw the
strange meal safely transported, and the men came to the table
and made no remarks about anything out of place, to Christina's intense relief. Mark got some glasses out of the cupboard, and a bottle of port, which he poured out all around
while Russell carved the joint. Christina sat down timidly.
The glass before her was brim-full, and the large plate swam
with thick cuts of the greasy meat.

"Cut the bread," Russell said to her.

They all ate, fast and hungrily, in silence. Christina, reliev-
ing this trembling emptiness inside her, felt a marvelous release, because no one criticized. No one told her to sit up, wipe
her mouth, put her knife and fork properly. Russell and Mark
ate with their heads down, mopping plates with hunks of torn
bread, and washing the meat down with gulps of port. Christina did not touch her port, until Russell said gruffly, as he
refilled his own glass, "Drink up, girl. Good for the blood."
The table was lit with white candles; after a few sips of the
port, Christina felt mellow, almost happy. The tight spring
of fear inside her unwound. "How strange it is," she kept
thinking. The hunting talk was resumed after the initial hunger
was appeased, and it swam around her head: draws and casts
and checks and points. She saw how the old man came out of
his surliness, and nodded eagerly at Mark's comments, his face
for the first time showing a light of pleasure. It was as if he
could not hear enough, drawing out Mark's opinions and descriptions. Mark, flushed with wine, started making diagrams
with bread crumbs on the polished table, of a clever move on
the fox's part, but he was interrupted in this demonstration
by a knock at the door.

"Come in!" Russell bellowed.

The doctor came in, a bit apprehensively Christina thought.
"Have a glass of port," Russell said. "Get a glass, Mark."

The doctor sat down with a nod of thanks.

"How is he? All right?" The animation had left Russell's
face.

The doctor shrugged. "It will be a long job, and whether it will heal without leaving its mark, I cannot say."

"You mean there'll be two lame ducks in the family?"

"I hope not, sir."

"Hmm." William's disaster seemed to affect his father more with anger and contempt than sympathy. "The boy's only himself to blame. The horse jumped clean enough, according to Mark. I bought Woodpigeon off that parson at Knowsley, especially for William. The animal is as sage as they come— bold, I'll say that for him, but clever. And looks after himself. Which is more than you can say for the boy. I don't know where Will gets it from, Porter. There's never been a Russell that rode as badly as William. Why, even the women rode better. His mother would have thought nothing of a place like that, and my sisters—they took everything as it came. Even this girl here, if she's anything like Hetty—" His bloodshot eyes, full of pain and drink and disappointment, wandered to Christina, and rested on her face.

"Can you ride? Your Aunt Grace teach you?"

"No, sir. I've never ridden."

"Good God, girl. What an admission! We'll have to remedy that. That mare would suit her, Mark, the strawberry roan. Sweetbriar. She's gentle. You teach the girl to ride on Sweet-briar."

Mark made a face. "Me teach her? Surely Dick could teach her? I'll take her out when she's ready."

"Yes, all right. She can start with Dick tomorrow. You got anything to wear, child?"

Christina, mute with apprehension, shook her head.

"Stand up!" Russell said. "Let's look at you. Turn around. Hmm." He considered, as Christina did as she was told. "Plenty of flesh there. I reckon Isabel's old habit would fit you. Tell Mary to get it out and do whatever's necessary. Or get a dressmaker to do it. We might have you hunting by Christmas if we're lucky."

Christina stared at him. The whole room seemed to whirl around her head and come to rest again with an awful, horrid reality. She saw the men with the sheepfold gate, and William's

sweating white face, and those men on the road, all spat-
tered with mud.

"But—"

Russell's gaze stopped her. She knew then that everybody in
this house did as he said. Even poor William.

Some Reading for William

"Miss Christina, I should be much obliged—"said Mary, the housekeeper, with dark circles of weariness under her eyes— "Violet's got the fires to do, and Mr. Russell wants his breakfast . . . if you'd just sit with William for an hour or so, till he wakes."

Christina, washed and dressed and about to go downstairs, was only too pleased to defer another mealtime meeting with her uncle. "Yes, of course."

"I'll bring you your breakfast up, if you like. It would be such a help, dear . . ."

"Yes. I would like to do it." Anything, Christina was thinking, than ride a horse in Aunt Isabel's habit. Mary gave her an exhausted smile and hurried away down the stairs, and Christina cautiously opened the door of William's room. William's unconscious company appealed to her.

Whatever she had expected in evidence of William's tastes, it was not what confronted her when she looked in. The room was barely furnished, but hanging from the ceiling was a collection of model flying machines. In the draft from the door, wings of stretched, gauzy cloth gyrated delicately before her eyes, twisting on their cotton threads, like great suspended insects with strut and wire and thread for legs and antennae. Christina was so surprised she stood and stared. There were six of them, all intricate and absurd, and lovingly made, like

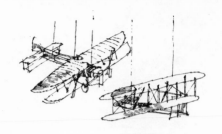

rare caged birds caught up in the prison of a boy's bedroom, wing tip to wing tip with the wardrobe and the bed head.

"Oh!" Her eyes went to the bed, and from the pillow a pair of dark eyes stared back at her, cool and curious.

"Are you Christina?"

"Yes." She shut the door and went and sat in the big chair pulled beside the bed. "I'm sorry about—about what's happened." She looked nervously at the bedclothes, which seemed to be heaped up in a queer way.

"I'm not sorry," William said. Then, "It's a fireguard."

"A fire—?"

"To keep the weight of the covers off my leg," William said.

"Oh." Christina felt very strange with William, who struck her at once as a very odd little boy, and as unlike Mark as a robin from a rook. He lay on his back, his black hair tumbled back from a face that was like a tracing of Mark's, with all the features similar, yet with the whole character of it different. Christina felt baffled.

She said, to try to get things tidier in her mind, "You're not sorry?" She could not see how he could fail to be sorry, to be stuck for weeks on his back, with only a fireguard for company.

"No more hunting," he said. "And Father can't climb the stairs, you know."

At once Christina understood. She had complete sympathy with the sentiments expressed so explicitly in the two sentences. She smiled warmly.

"Yes, I see." She paused. "You don't like hunting? I thought—"

"You thought all Russells liked hunting? Well, not this one. Doing this is like spring coming in November, as far as I'm concerned."

Christina, working it out, said, "Hunting stops in the spring, you mean?"

"Of course. My favorite time of the year."

"But do you have to, if you don't like it?"

"Yes," said William. "You've met my father?"

"Yes. I understand."

"Not only do you have to do it, you have to talk about it all the time," William explained. "You'll see, if you stay. Are you staying?"

"I think so."

"Good."

"He said last night that I have to learn to ride, and that I could be hunting by Christmas."

"Yes, of course. But you might like it. There's no accounting for taste. Look at Mark."

Christina thought, grimly, that she might fall off like William.

"What happened yesterday?"

"Oh, I don't know. I can remember the horse going flat gallop at a ghastly looking place, and that's all. I think I was probably so frightened I fainted in mid-air."

"Doesn't it hurt, though?"

"Not at this minute," William said. "But it does, on and off, quite a lot. But it's still worth it. Can't you ride, then? Have you never?"

"No. Uncle—your father—said I am to ride something called Sweetbriar. And Dick is going to teach me."

"Dick is nice. And Sweetbriar is as nice as it's possible for a horse to be, so I wouldn't worry. You might love it."

Christina settled thoughtfully in her chair, feeling that William was a big improvement on Mark. She looked at the flying machines, gently revolving in the November breezes, and the large hump of the fireguard under the bedspread. He was going to be a long time looking at his models.

"Did you make those?"

"Yes."

"Is it what you're interested in, instead of hunting? Flying machines?"

"Yes." William spoke very cautiously.

"Have you ever seen one?"

William did not reply. Christina said, "It is ridiculous, to think a man can fly. They will just get killed." She had heard it said at every house she had ever lived in.

"A man can fly," William said. "A man has flown. You don't know what you're talking about."

Christina was surprised. "No," she agreed. "I don't know anything about it. Only what people say."

"People have always ridiculed the great inventions. They have no imagination, always looking backward. Suppose no-

body tried to do anything that hadn't been done before? We should still be living in caves."

Christina, put in her place, nodded appeasingly. "Yes, of course."

"And motorcars . . . they work, don't they? People laughed at them, a few years ago."

"Yes."

"Father shouts about them, even now. And yet, if only he stopped to think, someone had to be the first to think of getting astride a horse."

"Yes." Christina looked at William cautiously, impressed by his intelligence. She hoped he would not be too intelligent for her; she did not relish the prospect of being despised by Mark for her ineptitude on horseback, and by William for her lack of imagination.

"Do—do you go to school?" she asked timidly, not having given the subject any thought before. William obviously had a scholarly nature.

"We have a tutor," William said. "On non-hunting days, that is. Tuesday and Thursday. He comes here. He's awful."

"Oh."

"He's always reporting us to Father, and about once a week there are big thrashings all around, me for insolence and Mark for rotten work. But I suppose it's better than some awful boarding school. You'll probably get on with him all right. I should think he's all right with girls."

"Why, am I to have lessons too?"

"If you want 'em, I suppose. After all, he's here dispensing knowledge. That's what he's paid for. You might as well soak a bit in, mightn't you?"

"Well, yes, if I'm allowed to."

"Allowed to? Nobody will tell you: you must decide for yourself. Father will only make you ride. He doesn't bother apart from that."

A spasm of pain crossed William's face, and his flippancy lapsed into a brooding silence that Christina did not like to disturb. Christina did not know whether the change of mood was due to pain or the gist of the conversation: there was obviously a great gulf between William's desires in life and what his father wished on him, and Christina felt sorry for him, in spite of his brains. She guessed that in schoolwork he would run rings around his brother, yet it was not schoolwork that mattered in this obsessed household.

Christina did not have long in which to ponder about how she would fare on the back of a horse. By ten o'clock, when Dr. Porter called again, Mary had ferreted out the dreaded habit, and Christina was in her room, trying it for size. To her dismay it fitted perfectly; in fact if she had been well-disposed toward the garments she would have noticed that the fine black cloth, long-skirted and tight-waisted, was extremely becoming. The black velvet cap sat snugly on her smooth hair. "At least, my brains are as big as Aunt Isabel's were, and she managed," Christina thought.

"Go and show Mr. Russell," Mary said, poking her head around the door. As usual, she was doing several jobs at once, waiting on Dr. Porter, supervising Christina, and preparing lunch between times. Christina went reluctantly along the passage, past the open door of William's room, where Dr. Porter was standing with his head among the flying machines, and down the stairs, skirt trailing, to Uncle Russell's lair.

He eyed her sharply from the leather armchair. "Hmm. Good. Go and get started then. Tell Dick I said to give you an hour every morning."

Christina hesitated, waiting for more explicit instructions, but Russell said, "Go on, girl. What are you waiting for?" so she backed out into the hall and went tentatively to the front door. If nobody was going to take her to the stables and introduce her to Dick, she supposed she was going to have to do it herself. Her heart sank, but she thought of William, and his saying that Dick was nice, and went out into the drive.

The morning was bright, a cold sunlight dispersing the hint of frost on the gravel, the view across the park blue and hazy with the smoke of autumn, the air tart to the nose. Christina's spirits rose immediately. The open air suddenly seemed a marvelously free and unbigoted thing, rich with the smells of wet earth and rotting crab apples, and quite free from the vibrations of human discord that Christina suddenly realized had been humming around her ever since she had set foot inside the door of Flambards. She gave a little skip to celebrate her sudden independence. "They're a lot of old women in there," she thought. "I won't get involved with their feuds. And I shall like riding, I'm sure." She had to admit that, with the sun shining, the tumbled countryside, damp and sparkling, that lay in wait all around the inconsequent brick walls of Flambards and its outbuildings was a far more inviting aspect than the rain-wet cobbles of Battersea High Street where Aunt Grace would now be waiting for a tram. Christina lifted her face to the damp air and said, "I like it. It is going to be all right."

The drive curved around under the chestnut trees and entered the stableyard under a handsome arch. The yard exuded an atmosphere of peaceful efficiency quite unlike the atmosphere of the house: Christina was aware of it at once. Everything was clean and shining, the gravel weeded, the paint fresh. The yard was not very big: it housed several horses, and there were four men to look after them. Christina was greeted with a quick courtesy that was in complete contrast to her welcome in the house the afternoon before. A little elderly man with a wrinkled face came up to her and said, "What can I do for you, miss?"

He was no taller than she was, and had a smile far brighter than any she had yet seen inside the house. Christina felt better and better.

"Mr. Russell said I was to ask Dick to give me a riding lesson," she explained.

"You're Miss Christina, I take it? Miss Hetty's young girl?"

"Yes."

"It's very nice to see you here, miss. I taught your mother to ride, you know, and Miss Grace. Fine straight riders they both were too. It will be a pleasure to have you riding our horses, miss, if I may say so. It's a long time since we've had a lady riding the horses, not since Mrs. Russell died."

Christina said anxiously, "I can't ride, you know. I might not be very good."

"We all have to start, miss. And Dick will put you right. He's a good boy, very patient. I'll get him to saddle Sweetbriar and you can look at the horses, miss."

Christina thought that they would all look the same to her, but thanked him politely. The man turned around and shouted, "Dick!" and a boy of about fifteen emerged from a doorway and came obediently across the yard.

"Saddle Sweetbriar for Miss Christina."

"Yes, sir."

Christina looked at the boy solemnly, feeling that a great deal depended upon Dick. He was a straight, well-built boy,

with hair the color of straw, and a brown skin, big brown
gentle hands, and an unhurried way of moving, very quiet and
measured, as if the world were full of fractious horses. He
nodded to Christina, flushing shyly, and made off toward the
tack room; and the old man said, "You'll learn fine with him,
miss. He's a very steady boy."

Christina was conducted around the stables and introduced
to the horses. She took particular note of Woodpigeon, who
had left William in the ditch, and Treasure, who had featured
so prominently in Mark's conversation the evening before.
They stared at her with purple-dark eyes in the cool, dimmed
light of the stable, tall, gentle, unfathomable to Christina. She
stood well back, impressed by the spotless floors, the fresh
straw all in place, the gleam on the horses' coats.

"How they shine!"

"Two hours strapping they get a day, Miss Christina, each
horse," said the old man. "The boys are all here by six."

Treasure put out an inquiring muzzle, curious, but ready
to jump away, his legs nervous in the straw. The groom put
up an arm and stroked his neck with a murmuring of nonsense.

"He's a new one, this. Very touchy, very funny in his ways.
Mr. Mark's trying him out." Treasure's coat was like damask,
a faint pattern of mottles glowing on the richness of his flanks
and shoulders. "He had a hard day yesterday."

Christina thought, "So did William." She looked respectfully at the big gray in the next box, and thought how small
William must have looked on top. The gray had a kind, quiet
face, with fatherly eyes.

"This is Woodpigeon?"

"That's right, miss. A fine bold jumper he is, and a nice
natured horse. I was right sorry to hear about Mr. William
yesterday, because I thought this horse would suit him. He's
not got the strength of Mr. Mark, hasn't Mr. William. I dunno
how it is, the pair of them brothers and yet so different. His
heart's not in it, I don't think."

Christina thought of the flying machines revolving from
William's ceiling, and shook her head in sympathy.

"Sweetbriar's ready, sir," Dick said from the doorway, and Christina followed the old groom, nervousness fizzing in her breast. Sweetbriar was large, and an extraordinary color. "Why, she's pink!" Christina exclaimed.

"Strawberry roan, we call it, miss," said the groom. Christina saw Dick grin, and wished she had kept quiet. To her relief, the mare was standing beside a stone mounting block, which would obviously see her most of the way up to the impressive sidesaddle. "If you look closely, you'll see it's gray and chestnut hair mixed. Mr. Mark calls her 'the pink mare'—he never has cared for her for some reason. Not enough spirit for him, perhaps. But she's a good horse, a very good horse. Eh, Dick?"

"Yes, sir."

"Step up here then, Miss Christina. I'll see you settled, then Dick can walk you around the paddock."

Gingerly, holding her skirt, Christina climbed the steps.

"Put your leg over the pommel. You'll see it's quite comfortable. In fact it's quite hard for a lady to fall out of a sidesaddle. Isn't that right, Dick?"

"Yes, sir."

Christina cautiously sat down, hitching her right leg over the pommel as instructed. It held her firmly, and she was agreeably surprised. The mare shifted legs, and Christina lurched. There was nothing to hold on to. But it was true that the pommel held her in place, hooking around her thigh, so that the rest of her leg hung forward against the horse's shoulder. The left leg was apparently to be supported by a stirrup, for the groom took hold of her foot and pushed it in.

"That's it now. Sit up straight. Sit square and face forward. Pick up your reins. Like this."

He showed her how to hold the single snaffle rein, and Dick went into the stable and fetched out another horse, saddled and bridled, which he mounted (without the aid of the mounting block) and brought to stand alongside Sweetbriar. The groom fixed a leading rein to Sweetbriar's bridle and handed it to Dick.

"There you are now. Half an hour will be enough, Dick, for the first time."

"Yes, sir."

The two horses moved forward side by side across the yard and out through a gate into a large paddock. The grass was short, yellowed with autumn, and sloped slightly uphill, and trees grew closely all around the fence, to give an inviting, private look to the field. At the top was the same wood Christina looked out on from her bedroom window, where the crows tumbled about the shriveling oak leaves. Christina fixed her eyes on it, between Sweetbriar's red ears, her hands rigidly held in front of her. The horse's movement, even at a walk, seemed very uncomfortable.

"You must give to it, miss," Dick said. "Not so stiff. And your hands must give. You want to feel the mare through your fingers, and your back."

Christina risked a glance at Dick, who sat all of a piece with the horse he rode, supple and easy, the reins in one hand, Sweetbriar's lead in the other. She saw immediately what he meant, but to do it, feel it, was not as simple as it sounded.

"It will come," Dick said simply.

Christina liked Dick's philosophy. She could see why Mark had given the job of teaching her to Dick, for Dick was solid, and kind, and immeasurably patient. They walked around and around the field, that morning and for every morning afterward, in the November sunshine, and in the wind and the rain, and through the still, gray half-mist, always the yellow grass underfoot and the woods full of crows all around. Sweetbriar was kind, and Christina began to feel her, and her mouth came up through the reins to Christina's fingers, so that she knew when she had to give to her, and when to hold her. Always Dick was sitting beside her, very still and quiet, a slow smile encouraging her.

When she went back to the house from the stables, she was forcibly struck by the contrast between the orderly, well-manned stableyard, and the chaotic slovenliness of the house, where the old foxhounds shed their white hairs and Mary was always two jobs behind. Violet, very quiet and slow, and only a year older than Christina, did and redid the chores that came every day: the fires, the vegetables and the beds and slops and kerosene lamps. And Mary cooked and waited on Russell, who rang for her constantly, at all hours of the day and night, to fetch and carry for him, far more trouble than the invalid William, who lay in bed making another aeroplane, humming softly to himself.

"How are you getting on?" William asked Christina, when she took up his dinner. "Do you like it?"

"Well, so far," Christina admitted. "Dick makes it seem very easy. He doesn't get cross."

"Dick rides better than anybody," William said. "It's a terrible waste."

"What do you mean, a terrible waste?"

"Well, just being a servant. On hunting days he takes Mark's second horse, and meets him, and brings his first horse back. It's all hanging about, and getting cursed for not having the horse in the right place when it's wanted, and then riding back when everyone else is hunting. I mean, I don't like hunting, but everyone else seems to, and I jolly well bet Dick wouldn't half like to hunt, instead of waiting on old Mark."

Christina was surprised, not having looked at it that way. "I thought he liked his job."

"Oh yes, I dare say he likes it as much as any he could get. But when you think of it, it's a bit like being a horse yourself, having to do exactly as you're told."

"Why, yes . . ." Christina considered. "But you have to, too," she ventured.

"Yes, now I do, curse it. But not when I'm a bit older. Then I shall do as I please. But Dick never will."

Christina thought that William had extraordinary ideas. She looked at the books that lay on the bed: one was called *Aerodynamics* and the other *Progress on Flying Machines*.

"What will you do then?"

"Fly," William said.

In the afternoon Mark asked her how she was getting on, and Christina answered as she had answered William.

"I'll take you out soon," Mark said, "if you like."

"Thank you," Christina said, with a sinking of the heart.

"You get on all right with Dick?"

"Oh, yes, of course. He's very good with me. He never gets cross."

"I would," said Mark, grinning. He was sitting at the bottom of the stairs, fondling one of the smelly foxhounds, the white hairs all over his breeches. He always wore very old, dog-smelling clothes in the house, a Norfolk jacket with leather elbows and frayed cuffs, which he did not even change for dinner. But three days a week, on hunting mornings, he appeared in immaculate hunting clothes, with shining boots, spotless breeches, and the beautiful scarlet jacket. On those mornings even Dick wore a black jacket and velvet cap, and left immediately after Christina's lessons to take Mark his second horse. If the meet was far away, Christina had no lesson, for Dick had already left.

"Dick rides very well," Christina said loyally.

"Yes, for a groom," Mark said. "Has he got you cantering yet?"

"I have a few times."

"Father reckons you could be out with hounds by Boxing Day, if you're any good. You'd learn fast then, faster than just hacking about."

Christina did not reply. She began to experience how William felt hounded by the old man's obsession; already at dinner, he was drawing her into the conversation, asking her about the lessons, which she would have enjoyed more if she had not felt she was being forced to gratify Russell's passion. She was expected to follow Mark's post-mortems on hunting days, to understand the terms and make sensible remarks. If she kept silent Russell would bark at her, "And what have you got to say, eh? Looking forward to your first meet? Get her blooded by the New Year, eh, Mark?" Christina swallowed; the term made her feel sick. ("What does it mean, blooded?" she asked Dick, and Dick said, "They smear a bit of the fox's blood on your forehead, that's all. It's nothing.")

Russell would keep looking at her with his hard eyes, and say, "Your mother rode well. She rode hard. And she was only a little thing." Christina was never at ease with her uncle, not at dinner, when she had to think hard to say the right things, nor during the day when he dragged his mangled legs about the big library, looking for his tobacco, or a book, or shouting for Mary to fetch something, always restless and rough-voiced. He drank a lot, and turned pages of books—books on hound breeding and horse racing. He dozed, snoring coarsely, then woke with a shout for the fire to be made up, or the lamps to be lit. He was never serene, and only happy when Mark was fresh home, mud-splattered and sweaty, to describe the day's hunting. Then they would dine, and drink port and talk endlessly about every move and every incident, and Russell's dark eyes would flame with excitement. He would even laugh. Twice Mark fell asleep before he left the table, exhausted with the day's riding and the reriding over dinner, and Russell laughed and said proudly to Christina, "The young puppy! Ridden himself unconscious."

When Christina told Dick, Dick said shortly, "Yes, he's

ridden his horse into the ground too. If he had to care for
Treasure when the day was over, he'd think twice at how he
carries on. It was midnight last night before I could get the
horse to settle. Not worth going home—I slept with him in
the end. Even Mr. Russell never rode his horses like that."

"What happened to Mr.—Uncle—Russell?" Christina asked.

"Horse fell on him," Dick said. "Three years ago. They
thought he'd die. All smashed up he was. It's a wonder how
he can move at all."

"And did he hunt all the time then?"

"Yes. He owned the pack then. The kennels were here. He
did as he pleased, and wonderful sport he showed. The old
place was really alive then. There were fifteen horses here, as
well as the kennels, and the hunt servants all lived here, in
the cottages behind the stables."

Christina had seen the forlorn cottages behind the stables,
with the ivy growing over the windows and the willow herb
pushing up through the brick paving. Sometimes they rode
that way, past the cottages and into the big home wood with
its tangled rides, Flambards Covert.

"He was always in the kennels or the stables, your uncle,"
Dick said, "when he wasn't hunting. Or else riding around
the farm. He had two hundred acres and knew what was happening on every inch of it. The home farm—that's the other
side of the covert; it's all in ruins now—there were twelve
horses there, besides a herd of Shorthorns. Six Shires and six
Clydesdales. My father was the horseman there, before he
died."

"Who farms the land now, then?" Christina asked.

"Oh, it's let off to Mr. Allington. He's got all the neighbor-
ing land. But he's not like your uncle was, you can see the
difference."

"And the hounds?"

"Mr. Lucas took them. He had new kennels built at his
own place—it's five miles away from here—and the hunt servants moved over there with him. He shows good sport; he's
all right. But it's all different here now, nothing like it was."

Christina pondered, her eyes on Sweetbriar's red ears. No wonder Uncle Russell's eyes were full of the restless agony that set her on edge.

"He had the energy of six, did Mr. Russell. He missed nothing: hunting, racing. He was always a hard man to work for. He expected every man to be as strong as he was. He used to lay about men who displeased him. He always had a wild temper, even then."

Christina could well imagine. Mark had had three canings for various misdemeanors since she had lived in the house, and no doubt William would be in for his share when he came downstairs again. She had an uneasy feeling that he would not be above giving her a cut or two if she angered him. But now she understood his great restlessness, his dreadful disgust with the failed body that he dragged about the library.

"But now . . . is there nothing for him? He never goes out at all. Couldn't he drive around, and see the horses, or go to the meets, if it means so much to him?"

"We tried that, miss. When he was walking again, Dr. Porter said to get a float—it's low to the ground you see. Mr. Russell was going mad with boredom, he said. So we thought at least he could see hounds, from the float, and go around the farms. But when we got it around to the door, when he came to get in, he couldn't do it. He has to use his arms for the crutches, so he had nothing to pull himself with. Even with two men helping, it was no good. He fell on the gravel, and cut his face. And he lay there and laid about him with his crutches, raging he was, and crying—the tears falling down his face. And he never tried again."

Christina was appalled. She could picture it so vividly: Uncle Russell's shattered pride, and the bull-like frustration that made him lash out with the very crutches that were his humiliation. No wonder that he had never tried again! A gentle, patient man, damaged even as gravely, would have succeeded, but the great bull that was Uncle Russell could not bring himself to face such a hurdle again. She looked at Dick, the horror still in her eyes, but Dick smiled and said, "There, Miss Christina, don't fret. There's men worked for him, day in, day out, and never had as much pleasure in all their lives as he got in one day before his accident." If there was any more meaning in this remark than a mere wish to soothe, Christina did not notice it just then. Later, the remark was to come back to her.

When they rode back into the stableyard, Mark was waiting for them.

"I just came to see if Treasure was all right," he said casually. "Mr. Russell wants to see you, Dick. He told me to tell you."

"Yes, sir."

"Did Treasure feed all right?"

"Yes, sir. Eventually."

"What do you mean, eventually?" Mark spoke roughly to Dick, and in his voice Christina heard her uncle, as if it had been he standing there. She was suddenly struck, with Russell so much in her mind, by the similarity, by Mark's physical presence, proud and strong, as Russell's must have been once. It was arrogance, she thought, an almost brutal presence that Mark had; she could see how Russell had bullied his servants, as Mark was now bullying Dick.

"I didn't get him dry till midnight. He kept breaking out. Very restless he was," Dick said.

"Oh, he's a fool horse," Mark said. "And if you'd had Woodpigeon waiting where you should have been, I wouldn't have had to carry on with him, would I!"

"No, sir," said Dick, very evenly.

"Where did you get to?"

"I was at Meadgate when Mr. Lucas put hounds into the new covert."

"Why didn't I see you, then?"

"You never looked," Dick said.

"Don't be a fool!" Mark said angrily. "I'm not blind. If you'd been there, I would have seen you."

Dick's face colored up. "I—" He stopped immediately, with a great effort, and stood silent, twisting his horse's reins in his hands.

"You mind your tongue." Mark said. "Or you'll go."

"Yes, sir."

Dick turned away abruptly, to help Christina dismount. She slipped down, steadied by Dick's arm, and saw the anger in his mild face. It hurt her, and she realized that, although Dick was only a servant and had to expect such treatment, he was more of a friend to her than Mark. She had learned to speak quite easily with him on their rides, far more easily than she had yet spoken with anyone up at the house.

"I'll wait for you, if you've got to come up to the house," she said to him.

"I'll just put the horses away, miss," Dick said.

He led the two horses into the stables and Mark said to Christina, coldly, "He knows the way. What are you waiting for?"

"What does Uncle want to see him for?" Christina asked, to avoid the question.

"I suppose he wants to know how you're getting on." He looked at her crossly. "D'you only ride Sweetbriar?"

"Yes, so far."

"Any fool can ride that horse. It's time you tried something else. I'll tell you what—it's hunting tomorrow, but the next day, Thursday, I'll take you out instead of Dick. We can go a good long hack, then I'll be able to tell Father myself how you are."

Christina hoped she did not look as unwilling as she felt. She said nothing.

Mark said, slyly, "If you're no good, Dick will get into trouble. He's had long enough at you."

"All right, you'll see!" Christina said indignantly. "No one could have taught me better. If I'm no good, it's my own fault, none of Dick's."

When Dick was ready they walked back to the house, Dick following behind. They went into the hall and Mark went to the library door and shouted in, "Here's Dick, Father." Dick had taken his cap off and stood nervously twisting it in his hands, his pale golden hair surprising Christina, for she had never seen him without a cap. Russell shouted, "Come here then, all of you!" and they filed in, Mark first. Russell sat glowering from his leather chair, his shrunken legs stretched out before him and the crutches hooked over a knob in the ornate carving of the mantelpiece.

"Well, Dick, come here, boy. Stand where I can see you. How's Miss Christina getting on? That's what I want to know. Is she ready to go out with Mr. Mark yet?"

"She could go out with him steady, sir. She's coming along very nicely."

Christina watched Russell, seeing him flailing his crutches on the gravel drive and crying with disappointment. She was fascinated, watching his sharp, sunken eyes on Dick and the deep lines of bitterness around his mouth. He must have ridden like a lion, she thought, with his craggy face lit up with excitement, his hounds tumbling all around him.

"Has she jumped yet?"

"Not yet, sir."

Russell frowned.

"It's only three weeks, sir," Dick said.

The Russells did not understand patience, Christina thought. None of them had Dick's essential kindness.

"Well, she's not a ninny," Russell said, his eyes switching to her sharply.

"No, sir. I dare say she could jump now, if you wish."

"I want her hunting this season, not next. Remember that. And, Dick, this new horse, Treasure. How is he? Is he a good doer?"

Dick looked wary. "He's very nervous in the stable, sir. Very finicky."

"Improving? Or not?"

"He's settling a bit, sir." Dick glanced at Mark, and Christina remembered what Dick had said about Mark's riding the horse into the ground. Mark was looking at Dick too, daring him to tell the old man.

"He's worth taking trouble with," Russell said. "He'll win races that one. You see he has the best."

"Yes, sir."

"All right." Russell dismissed Dick. Christina went to the door with him, and was surprised to find a man standing there, pressing the doorbell.

"Mr. William Russell live here, miss?"

"Yes."

The man handed her a parcel. "With the regards of Mr. Dermot," he said and, touching his cap, walked away down the drive.

Christina took the parcel back into the library and handed it to her uncle. "A man delivered this, with the regards of Mr. Dermot."

"Who the devil's Mr. Dermot?" Russell said, with a glare at the parcel.

"He didn't say."

"Open it, girl."

Christina did as she was told, and was shocked by her own stupidity. For the parcel was a book called *A Scientific Statement of the Progress of Aeronautical Science up to the Present Time*, and on the flyleaf a small hand had written, "To help while away the time." It was for William upstairs, not his father.

She said, "It's for William."

"Show me," said Russell.

Christina handed it over reluctantly. She had a feeling that William would have preferred to keep his reading matter private. Russell stared at the title.

"Good God, what's this stuff?"

Mark leaned over the back of the chair to read the cover, and laughed. "That's Will's passion. Flying."

"*Flying!*" Russell was disgusted. He opened the book and read the inscription. "I'll give him something to while away his time! I've never seen him show any interest in my books, the brainless puppy! Who is this Dermot, filling his head with rubbish? Eh, Mark? You know him?"

"Never heard of him," said Mark.

"Holy Moses, if he wants to while away his time—" Russell

was thumping about, stumbling over to the bookcase, red with anger— "I'll give him something. Here, Christina, take these out. I'll give him reading matter. Take this up to him, and this one. Here. And this."

Christina took the awkward tomes, silent with horror. They were *The Breeding of Foxhounds, Baily's Hunting Directory, Observations on Foxhunting, Thoughts on Hunting, The Essex Foxhounds,* and *Goodall's Practice With Foxhounds.*

"Take him those! Go on! With my compliments. I'll see he gets his reading matter. And when he's finished those I'll send him some more." He took the slim volume on flying and threw it on the fire, where it burst into merry flames. Christina could not restrain a gasp of dismay, and even Mark looked disconcerted.

"Oh, I say, Father."

Russell aimed a great swipe at Mark with his crutch, which Mark avoided with a quick, practiced sidestep.

"Get out, both of you! Get upstairs with those, girl, and tell

Will to start reading. Get out of my sight before I tan the
hides off you!"

He was scarlet with passion, crashing his crutches in the
hearth, poking the flying book deeper into the fire. Christina,
clutching her load of books, hurried out, and Mark opened the
door for her, grinning.

"Phew! What a storm!"

Once in the hall, Christina burst into tears. She could not
wipe her eyes for the books, and stood gulping uncontrollably.
"It's—it's not fair! The—the—book was for—for Will! It's all
—my fault!"

"Oh, Will's used to it," Mark said. "Don't upset yourself,
we're always like this here. You just have to keep out of the
old man's way till he's over it."

To her amazement, Mark was not the least concerned. Christina was outraged, and horrified by her own part in the matter.
It need never have happened at all, if she had not been so
dull-witted. Her heart ached for poor helpless William as she
lugged the books up the stairs. Mark had already washed his
hands of the incident and gone out of the front door with the
foxhounds at his heels. Christina's sense of injustice choked
her. She fumbled for William's doorknob, and backed into the
room with her burden, the sobs still shaking in her throat.

"Whatever's all that?" William asked cheerfully.

"For—for you!"

"What's the matter? What's wrong?"

Christina set the pile of books on the chair beside William's bed, and told him what had happened. As she had expected, William's rage turned itself on her. She buried her
head in the bedclothes and sobbed: "I'm sorry! I didn't know
he was so awful!"

"Oh, look, I'm sorry too," William said, immediately embarrassed by her despair. "It wasn't your fault. Oh, look, please
don't cry, else I shall too."

He gave her a white, desolate look, biting his lip with disappointment. His glance passed on to the gold-tooled hunting
books, and a look of utter contempt came into his face.

"If he thinks I'm going to read that rubbish! I'd— I'd like to tear them into shreds! If only I had the nerve—"

"Oh, William, don't make it worse! Don't be so stupid!"

Christina pulled herself together and wiped her eyes. William lay back, glaring at the ceiling, his lips tight. His face was very pale, and there were dark shadows under his eyes. Christina said nervously, "Who is Mr. Dermot, then?"

"A friend," said William distantly.

Later that evening Russell sent a message up to William to the effect that when he came downstairs, he was going to answer questions on the hunting books, and if he could not answer correctly, he would get a flogging, smashed knee or no smashed knee. William picked up *Baily's Hunting Directory* and threw it across the room, where it landed under the washstand, half its leaves bursting out across the floor.

A Ride With Mark

The incident of Mr. Dermot's book weighed on Christina. As she went to bed that night she heard, for the first time, William sobbing. His door was open, and a nightlight burned, but she did not go in. She could not face him again, with the knowledge that the whole beastly thing was her fault. She lay in bed, and the winter moon shone coldly on the mottled wallpaper, and whitened the rampaging garden below. In the morning the long grass would be a fretwork of silver webs, and a cold fog would roll across the fields where she was to ride with Mark. She dreaded riding with Mark. She thought of Aunt Grace, and the ordered life she had lived with the dressmaking and lessons at Miss Peasgood's and tea in front of the fire, with the blinds drawn, and nobody to shout and argue and coerce.

"They are all mad here," she thought, "in different ways." Mark, who could be so amiable at times, and yet so rough, was two years older than she was, yet seemed a whole generation older. "He fits in here," she reflected. "But William . . ." William would never fit in. William was doomed, Christina thought, to struggle. She thought he would lose; he was so delicate. He had stopped crying, but from his room came a thump, and then a shuffling noise. "What is he doing?" she wondered, straining her ears. Silence. William was thirteen,

but a child compared to Mark. "And what am I?" Christina thought, seeing herself as someone who had learned to fit in, wherever she was put, uncomplaining, forced to adapt. Always she had done as she was told, having been threatened more than once (but never by kind Aunt Grace) that if she was a nuisance she would go to the orphanage. Was she really going to stay at Flambards, and marry Mark? Aunt Grace had written, but said nothing about her going back.

Christina lay looking at the moon, thinking of the long years ahead of her in the troubled atmosphere of Flambards. "It's better than an orphanage," she thought. And Mark would make a very handsome husband. And then, suddenly she remembered Dick, dear, kind Dick who was always nice to her, and she thought, "What a pity I can't marry Dick." She fell asleep, and did not hear the thumping and shuffling that went on in William's room, and the muffled, painful sobbing.

Two days later Mark took her out. She rode Sweetbriar and Mark rode Treasure, his favorite, who was nervous and sweating. Dick led the horses out and held Sweetbriar while Christina got into the saddle. He held her stirrup for her, patted the mare's neck, and said softly, "Have a good ride, miss."

Christina wanted to tell him that she would rather be going with him, but decided it would be out of place. Dick went to Mark, to tighten Treasure's girths, and the horse stood for him, flitching his long, nervous ears. Mark looked down on Dick from the saddle and said, "Don't be all day." He wore a black jacket and black cap, and sat very easily, his reins all in one hand. Christina felt worried, and tried to sit her best and look confident.

"Come on," Mark said.

Sweetbriar moved off to Christina's heel, and Treasure pranced past her, rattling his bit, a white rim showing around his eyes. Mark turned in his saddle and laughed. "What a horse, eh? You wouldn't think he galloped ten miles yesterday, would you? I reckon Father's right when he says he'll be winning races in a year or two's time."

Christina nudged Sweetbriar into a trot to keep up, and Mark watched her critically.

"Sit square, hands still. That's better."

Unaccountably, Christina felt furious, although she had never minded Dick's instruction. She stared crossly between Sweetbriar's ears and wondered why Mark let Treasure proceed at a crabwise jogging pace, instead of making him walk or trot properly. From Dick, she had learned that this was a bad habit in a horse, but Mark, allowing bad habits himself, criticized her. Christina raged, her lips tight.

"Not bad," Mark said. "Let's see you canter."

Treasure was off at a bound, fighting his bit, the sweat gathering on his neck. Christina had to admit that Mark sat him beautifully, very strong and yet graceful in the saddle, completely master of the difficult horse. She let Sweetbriar go, dear Sweetbriar whom she could always trust to look after her —and the mare went easily, light on her bit, ignoring the headstrong youngster raking along at her side, fighting for his head.

"Why, you're not bad at all," Mark shouted, sounding quite surprised, and Christina's anger changed to a hot glow of pride.

She did not let her expression change, but thought, "Nice Dick. You are all right, I've saved you."

She steadied Sweetbriar as they came to a gate, and Mark brought Treasure to a halt with a cruel pressure on the curb.

"Honestly, he's a mad horse," Mark said. "You wait here, and I'll show you what he can do, get the tickle out of his toes. He'll be all right when he's run it off a bit."

He turned Treasure sharply on his hocks and went off at a fast canter away from Christina across the field. Christina watched him go, glad that Sweetbriar was content to stand, mildly switching her ears to the winter crying of the rooks. Mark made for a low part of the cut-and-laid fence and Treasure flew it with scarcely a change in his stride, and continued at a gallop across the field beyond.

"Show-off," Christina thought. She had never been left alone on a horse before. The air was cold and clear, and she felt confident. She looked down at her gloved hands on the reins, quiet and firm, and the frosted neck of the mare shining with her two hours' daily polishing. She thought of the spotless stables, and the great feeds the horses got, and wondered if Dick and the others lived in anything like the same luxury as the horses they cared for. Dick, in spite of his stocky frame, was thinner than he should be, and had been coughing recently. If a horse coughed, it was rested and given stuff out of a bottle and invalid gruel with an egg beaten in it, but when Christina had said to Dick, "You ought to stay by a fire with a cough like that," he had looked at her in amazement and said, "But I couldn't stay off work, miss." "Why not?" Christina had asked, but Dick had only laughed, rather bitterly. Christina thought, "I ought to know about the servants. I don't know anything." She thought that when you lived in a big house in the country, you were supposed to go around and give food and clothes to the poor, but how could she do it when she was so poor herself? Her thoughts had wandered far away from Mark and Treasure by the time they reappeared, still galloping, back over the cut-and-laid fence and, more soberly, back to Sweetbriar's side. Mark's eyes were sparkling.

"There, that's satisfied him, eh? He'll go easily enough now."

Treasure certainly looked quieter, breathing easily through his distended nostrils. He was in superb condition, his coat gleaming like the dining-room mahogany.

"Look, you ought to try him," Mark said. "You've never ridden a proper horse yet. I don't know what Dick's thinking of."

"What do you mean, a proper horse?" Christina said indignantly. "What's wrong with Sweetbriar?"

"You know what I mean," Mark said. They were walking side by side across the field to the gate in the corner. "You ought to ride all sorts. You'd feel a difference, I can tell you."

"I don't want to ride Treasure."

"Are you afraid?" Mark asked cruelly, smiling.

"No, of course not. But if Dick thought I was up to riding Treasure he would probably have let me by now."

"Oh, Dick, Dick, Dick! He's only a servant. What does he know? Don't be so stupid. Come on, I'll change the saddles over for you, and you try him. I tell you, it'll be an experience for you—you'll be able to tell Father."

Christina hesitated. She felt doubtful about riding Treasure, but not afraid. Mark pulled up. "Come on. You ought to be jolly proud I'll let you."

Christina had no alternative but to get down. She held the horses while Mark changed the saddles over, then Mark gave her a leg up onto Treasure.

"Oh, all these reins!" Christina said, confused. She felt nervous now, looking at the very different neck in front of her, and the white rim of Treasure's eye.

"Look, you should learn. These are the snaffle reins, and these the curb. You hold them like this." He showed her. "There, that's right."

He mounted Sweetbriar, and looked at her critically. "Don't jab him with the curb, or he'll show you he doesn't like it."

Christina did not feel very happy. She was not afraid, she told herself. But Treasure was all spirit, even as he walked, she could feel it inside him; it quivered in her fingers as he tossed his head, pulling at the reins. He started to dance, moving along at the jog, instead of a walk. Mark laughed. Suddenly a gun went off in the woods behind them and Treasure gave a great leap forward. Christina, carried by the pommels beneath her thighs, was lifted with him, not even losing a stirrup. She heard Mark laugh again, and cry, "Hold him! Hold him!" But Treasure did not want to be held. He reached out his neck and pulled the reins through her fingers, and then he was galloping, and Christina knew that she was on her own.

She was not afraid, immediately. The sheer exhilaration of the horse's speed thrilled her, but his strength was ominous.

When she looked down she saw his shoulders moving with the smooth rhythm of steam pistons; she saw his black, shining hoofs thrown out, thudding the hard turf, and felt the great eagerness coming up through her own body. She knew that she could never stop him, if he decided he did not want to stop. She saw the hedge ahead of them, and the first stab of real fear contracted her stomach. She gathered her reins up tight, and pulled hard. It made no difference at all.

"Don't panic," she thought, but the panic was in her, whether she wanted it or not.

Treasure's stride lengthened as he approached the hedge. Christina, remembering William, shut her eyes and buried her hands in Treasure's mane, and the horse surged beneath her. There was a cracking noise of breaking twigs. Christina gasped, clutched, and gasped again, but to her amazement they were galloping again, the incident behind them, and she still in place. She let go of Treasure's mane and pulled on his mouth again, with all her strength, but he had the bit firmly between his teeth and she could make no impression. A great despair filled her.

"I shall be killed," she thought.

Treasure was turning to the right across another large, yellow field. Beyond it was the home paddock where Christina had taken her safe, enjoyable lessons with Dick. It dawned on her that the horse was making for home, but between the field they were in and the home paddock there was a hedge, very much larger than the one they had just jumped, solid and newly layered all along its length, and a good five feet high. Christina knew that Treasure was not the horse to be stopped by such an obstacle; she knew that he was going to jump it, and, by the grace of God, so was she. A great sob of despair broke from her throat.

"Treasure, don't! Don't, don't!" She leaned back on the reins, trying to saw the horse's mouth, but she could do nothing.

The creak of leather beneath her, the heavy thrumming of the horse's hoofs, filled her ears, which ached with the cold

wind. Her hair flew behind her. The horse, never tiring, galloped on, raking out with his flying hoofs.

Suddenly, in the mist of her watery vision, Christina saw
a gray horse come into sight at the top of the field. It was
cantering toward her, but circling slightly in such a way that it
looked as if it would come around and join her on her own headlong course. Christina thought it was Mark, impossibly flown
to save her. She lifted her head, and screamed into the wind,
"Help me! Please help me!" The hedge was getting rapidly
closer, and she started to cry out with fear, half sob, half
entreaty. Treasure's strength grew with every stride.

The gray horse, very much under control, had now circled
so that he was on the same course as her, but ahead and to
her right. As Treasure galloped on, the gray horse's stride
lengthened to match, and quite suddenly Treasure was galloping with his nose close by the gray horse's side. They were
both galloping, and Christina heard a voice shout, "Hold tight,
Miss Christina!" The gray was hard against Treasure's shoulder,
its rider's leg crushed against the sweat-shining machinery of
the gallop. Treasure was forced off course, ridden off by the
gray, and Dick was leaning over to take his reins, his face
puckered with anxiety.

"Hold hard!"

Christina felt the horses sliding, skidding, the great gallop
broken up into a series of jolts and crashes, Treasure berserk
beneath her. Strips of turf peeled up under his hoofs. Dick
was pulled up out of his saddle, and hung for a moment,
precariously straddled between the two horses, then at last
Treasure dropped his jaw and pulled up and Dick, still holding on, half fell and half jumped from his saddle, staggering
and swearing.

"You great ruddy brute! You devil you!" But as Treasure
pulled up he was stroking his neck, gentling him and swearing
at the same time; then he came around to Christina's side and
lifted her down. Christina's legs had no strength in them and
she stumbled against him.

"Dick! Oh, Dick!" she wept, and Dick tried to comfort her, with Treasure plunging around in circles on one hand, and Woodpigeon, the gray, sidling about on the other. Dick was full of indignation.

"Oh, Miss Christina, he shouldn't ever have put you on Treasure. He must be out of his mind. Steady on, my old beauty!"—this to Treasure, who was now beginning to quieten—"And you riding not a couple of months yet! There, miss, it's all right now."

Being spoken to as if she were a horse had a soothing effect on Christina, and she found that she was able to stand without her knees shaking. She wiped the mud and tears off her face and looked around dubiously.

"It was very clever of you to stop him, Dick," she said. The thorn hedge was some thirty yards away, and even nastier than she had supposed. There was a big drainage ditch on the take-off, newly dug, with the earth thrown out all along its lip. "What do you think would have happened if—?" Christina knees started shaking again. "I don't think I shall like hunting," she said. She thought of having to report to Uncle Russell that she had flinched at the big hedges and gone through the gates, and Mark would tell him that she was no good.

"Only a fool would put at a hedge like that, miss, even out hunting. You mustn't get afraid now, because of this. You sat him a treat. There, my old fellow, my old boy. You take it easy now." He had Treasure quite quiet, lipping at his fingers. "This horse isn't bad, miss. He's only young. He needs steady riding, not like he gets with Mr. Mark."

"Where is Mark?" Christina said.

"Coming now, miss."

Christina was furious with Mark, now that her fright was over. Mark cantered slowly up on Sweetbriar, looking very unconcerned. But when he pulled up beside them and looked at them both, Christina could see that he was afraid, and angry, but did not want to show it. He laughed and said to Christina, "Well, how about that for a gallop? Did you enjoy it?"

"He'd have gone through that hedge if Dick hadn't stopped him," Christina said coldly. "Then where would I have been?"

"Home by now," Mark said flippantly.

"She could have been killed, sir, and you know it," Dick said suddenly. "You had no right to put her on this horse."

"So you're taking credit for saving her life?" Mark said, his face flushing angrily.

"No. But I reckon it was lucky Mr. Fowler told me to take Woodpigeon out for an hour, that's all."

Mark got down from Sweetbriar and said to Dick abruptly, "Change the saddles back."

Dick did as he was told, silently. When Sweetbriar was ready he gave Christina a leg up, and Christina settled herself gratefully on the mare, and said, very gravely, "Thank you very much, Dick." She loved Dick very much at that moment, and hated Mark with a cold, flat contempt. Dick looked up at her and smiled one of his rare, sweet smiles.

"That's all right, miss."

Mark said to him, "Hold Treasure while I mount."

Dick soothed the bay horse, who sensed Mark's anger and was nervous again. When Mark had gathered up his reins, he paused and looked down at Dick.

"You won't mention what happened, when you get back?"

Dick said nothing. Mark flushed again, his anger rising. "You heard what I said? No one is to know what happened."

"If you say so, sir."

"Look," said Mark, very evenly, "I do say so. And I'll say something else. If I find out that anyone in the stables knows what happened this morning, I'll see that you get dismissed."

Dick's eyes opened very wide. He stroked Treasure's neck, silent, turning away from Christina.

"Well?"

"Yes, sir," Dick said. "I understand."

William's Decision

William listened solemnly to Christina's story.

"And, remember, you're absolutely not to mention a word of it to anyone, in case Dick gets into trouble," Christina said.

"*Dick* get into trouble!" William said. "He deserves a medal. I can tell you, I wish he'd been around the day I did this." William shifted irritably in the bed. "I know exactly how you felt, Christina. Nobody in the whole of Essex knows better, believe me. He must have been like the angel Gabriel himself swooping out of the sky."

"Yes," Christina agreed.

"Has it put you off?"

"What do you mean?"

"Do you want to go riding again?"

"Oh, of course. Why not? Sweetbriar is a dear."

William shook his head. "You're one of them," he said. "A proper Russell. No imagination. You just *fall* in the hedge next time, and find out what it's like. What's the point?"

"The point of what?"

"Oh, *Christina!*"

William could be very awkward, Christina thought. A fire burned in his room, and it was pleasant, when he was in a good mood, sitting watching the flying machines, and hearing the rain on the window, and feeling safe from Uncle Russell. There was a crash on the door, and Mark came in backward,

62

with a tray. It was very rarely that he came up to William's
room.

"Houseful of ruddy women, and I have to bring up your
supper," he grumbled. "Father's in a hell of a temper tonight."
He looked at Christina suspiciously. "What's she been telling
you, then? All about our little escapade this morning?" He
grinned suddenly, putting the tray down on William's stomach.
"She sat him jolly well actually. You'd have been off at the first
hedge."

"I wouldn't ever have got *on*." William pointed out.

Christina lifted the tray up and got William another pillow,
to make him comfortable. She looked at Mark warily. She
never knew what to expect of Mark. She thought he would
be furious to find out that she had told William the story,
but now he was laughing.

"You'd jolly well better not tell Father what happened,"
was all he said to William.

"I'm not likely to," William said.

"Did you mean what you said to Dick, about getting him
dismissed?" Christina asked Mark boldly. The viciousness of
his warning had stayed with her all day, and yet now Mark was
laughing, as if the whole incident had been funny. It had not
been funny just then, this morning, when Dick had turned
away.

"Of course I did," Mark said, as if there were nothing in it.

"But it was an awful thing to say."

Mark looked at her in amazement. "Why?"

Christina was shocked. "But it's—it's his *life*," was all she
could say.

"His job, you mean?" Mark laughed. "I can tell you, it
would be my life, if Father knew."

"Is that all you think of it?"

Mark looked exasperated. "What do you mean? What am I
supposed to think? I've a right to talk to him like that—what's
wrong about it?"

William looked at Christina sympathetically. "You won't
get him to understand," he said.

Christina said to William, "You understand then? What I mean?"

"Yes, of course."

"That he's a—a *person*. Not just a servant . . ."

"You're not used to having servants, obviously," Mark said. "You'll have to learn, if you're staying here. If you don't keep them in their place, you'd be surprised what would happen." He laughed, quite cheerful. He sat on the bed, and looked at the books lying on the covers. The titles amused him enormously.

"You are reading them, then? Good for you. We'll make a fox hunter of you yet."

Christina was surprised. "Are you reading them? I thought—" She had had the job of mending *Baily's Hunting Directory*, with the glue William used for his aircraft models.

"Look." William passed them a piece of paper. On it, in Russell's inelegant scrawl was written: "The first day you come downstairs you must know the breeding of every hound in my kennels, back to Harlequin, or twelve swishers. Also *Goodall's Practice with Foxhounds* by heart, or ditto. And answer questions on all other books, or ditto."

Even Mark was slightly daunted. "I say! By heart!" Then he added, "It's only short, though."

"Good heavens!" Christina was appalled. "But it's prose. It's not like learning 'Ye Mariners of England, That guard our native seas', or 'It was a summer's evening, old Kaspar's work was done.' "

"Father thinks *Goodall's Practice* is poetry," William said. "It's the way his mind works."

"Well, it's good stuff," Mark said.

William gave him a cold look. "You learn it then."

"I'm not getting swished," Mark pointed out.

William gave one great groan of exasperation and heaved himself impatiently on the pillows. Christina, feeling that he had every reason to groan, rescued his tray and said, "Don't you want this?"

"I suppose so."

When he had finished, Christina took the tray back to the kitchen. She had learned the house's routine now, and was gradually taking over some of the domestic duties, which she supposed Aunt Isabel must have once done. Mary the house-keeper now asked her opinion about things that needed doing, changing carpets around and washing curtains, and mending sheets, and sometimes about what meat to cook or pudding to make, and Christina liked the feeling that there was a place for her here. She had a dream of the house being all clean and gracious, with flowers in the hall, and no dirty foxhounds trailing around. In her vision Uncle Russell did not exist, and Mark was always gracious and polite. Visitors left calling cards and Violet opened the door in a black dress and frilly apron and said, "Yes, m'm," and did not wipe her nose on her sleeve. She wouldn't do it if she had on a stiff white cuff, Christina thought.

She took the tray into the scullery where Violet was wash-ing up. Violet was a very quiet girl, fair and pretty in a coun-try way, with her curly hair pinned back under a cap and her wide, unviolet-like green eyes. She had never spoken to Christina beyond a mumbled, "Yes, miss," and seemed always to be in the kitchen, although Christina knew she lived out. Mary was eating her supper.

"Has he eaten up?"

"Yes."

"He can do with it. He's getting very thin. And he was thin enough before."

"When will he be allowed up?" Christina asked, thinking of *Goodall's Practice.*

"I don't know, miss. Dr. Porter's not satisfied with his leg. He says it's not doing right, and he's not to walk on it yet on any account."

This news reassured Christina, thinking more of William's mammoth reading tasks than of his health.

"Poor little lad. It's right cruel making him ride those big horses out hunting. And after Mr. Russell's accident and all . . . you'd think one dose like that would be enough in the

house. I wouldn't be surprised to see Mr. Mark come home on
a stretcher one of these days either."

"Or me," Christina thought to herself. She remembered the
feel of Treasure's strength beneath her, and the cold wind
stinging her eyes. And Mark talking to Dick.

"Do you like Mr. Mark?" she said to Mary, curiously.

Mary was shocked. "Why, what a thing to ask, miss! Mr.
Mark is a fine young gentleman, for all his ways."

"Mr. Mark is very handsome," Violet said, in a low voice.
She picked up Mary's empty plate, and gave Christina a
straight, almost defiant look. Christina was surprised. It was
the first time she had heard Violet pass a remark, and this
particular remark seemed to her very daring.

"Wash the soup kettle. It's empty," Mary said to her
sharply, as if thinking the same thing. "And keep your mind on
your work."

Christina wished she had not spoken. Violet finished the
washing up and tidied everything away, then fetched her out-
door boots and shawl. It was dark outside and a thin drizzle
was falling.

"Good night, miss. Good night, m'm."

"Good night, Violet."

The girl went out, shutting the door quietly.

Christina sat by the kitchen fire and Mary made her a mug
of cocoa. She was thinking of the long, lonely driveway under
the fir trees, and the dark road to the village.

"Does Violet live in the village?"

"Yes, miss."

"I would not like to walk home in the dark."

"She's supposed to go in the daylight, but we're never done
in time this time of year. She'd live in, but she's got a sick
mother she can't leave."

Christina was thinking, "I ought to take her mother some
calves-foot jelly, and Bible pictures," but she knew she would
not dare. She wished she were older, and knew how to act,
and what to feel. Flambards was always surprising her. Life had

been much less confusing with Aunt Grace, who had rules for everything. Nobody seemed to have rules here. Even now, drinking cocoa in the kitchen with the housekeeper was not how Aunt Isabel must have spent her evenings, and yet with Christina it was what she did most often, because it was comfortable and away from Uncle Russell, who drank too much port.

She washed her mug in the scullery and took her candle to go to bed. Her room was ice cold and the wind rattled the window panes in their sockets. The candle wavered in the draft, and the shadows leaped about the faded wallpaper, but Christina, who had had more positive things than shadows to be afraid of during her lifetime, was not nervous. She remembered William saying she had no imagination. "Perhaps it is true," she thought. She climbed, shivering, into the icy bed and wrapped her nightgown tightly around her legs and ankles. But what good did it do William to lie and dream of flying machines, when his only opportunity for flying through the air was, like hers, from the back of an unmanageable horse? "If that's imagination," she thought, thinking of the airy models that would now be twisting in the draft like the candle flame, "he's welcome to it." Then she lay back and looked at the ceiling and thought, "No, that is not imagination. That is wishing. And everyone can wish." Uncle Russell wished for his legs, and William wished for his freedom. Christina turned and blew out her candle and fell asleep.

She was awakened some time later by a thud from across the passage. She listened, and heard the floorboards creak, and knew that the noise came from William's room. A light sleeper, Christina knew that, this time, she must investigate. Her curiosity was too great to let her go back to sleep.

She got up, lit her candle again and went out into the passage. The draft swirled up her legs, and she opened William's door quickly, and quietly.

The fire was glowing in the grate, and, outlined by its light, William stood in the middle of the floor between the end of

his bed and the hearth, quite unsupported. He was in his
nightshirt, and turned around at Christina's interruption with
a look on his face that made Christina cry out.

"William!"

Christina shut the door behind her and leaned on it, feeling
herself trembling all over.

"Whatever are you doing?" she hissed. "Are you mad?"

She set the candle down and went over to him, holding
out her arms. His face was a greenish color in the firelight, and
pinched up with pain, so that his eyes stood out as if twice
their usual size, blazing with a defiant agony that put Christina at a complete loss.

"What are you doing? Here, hold me!"

For a moment she thought he was going to fall. He swayed,
but half-turned away from her arms as if he would run from
her if he could. He took a staggering pace on the stiff broken
leg, half-cried out, and collapsed into the small chair in front
of the fire.

"William! What are you trying to do? Do you want something? You only had to call me!"

Christina dropped down on her knees beside him, horrified
by the ordeal he had inflicted on himself. His face was shining
with sweat, and he moaned, twisting himself in the chair,
turning his head away from her. Christina was frantic to help
him.

"William! Don't—don't—!"

She remembered the brandy bottle downstairs in the dining
room, and got up and ran, holding up her nightgown. In her
bare feet she sped down the stairs and across the hall to the
well-used sideboard where Uncle Russell's bottles stood shoulder to shoulder. His empty glass was still there. She grabbed
it and the brandy and ran back upstairs again. She remembered to shut the door, feeling that it was quite imperative
that no one else should know what was going on.

"Here, drink this."

She put her arm around William's shoulders and held the
glass to his lips. William resisted, shrinking from her like a

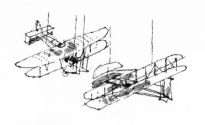

hunted rabbit, but Christina pushed the glass at him relent-
lessly.

"Here, you idiot! Or shall I fetch Mary?"

He drank the brandy at last, gasping and shuddering. Christina fetched a blanket from the bed and wrapped it around
him. He sat huddled in the chair, his broken leg in its plaster
stuck out into the hearth. Christina put another log on the
fire. William stared at the flames, his face stiff with some private
agony which Christina could not even guess at. It was no
longer a physical pain; it was something outside the realm
of Dr. Porter altogether.

"Are you all right?"

"Oh, stop fussing," he whispered angrily. "You didn't have to interfere, did you?"

"But what were you doing?"

"You could see, couldn't you? Just walking about."

"But *why*? However will your leg mend if you walk on it? You know what Dr. Porter said. What were you trying to do?"

Even as she asked the question Christina realized what was in William's mind. In the set, stubborn expression on his face, and by his very silence, she read the answer.

"You—you mean, that—that's what you want!" She was appalled. "Is—is—that why you—you—!" She stared at him, but he said nothing. "William, is it true?"

"I want it to set stiff, with the joint locked," William said. "Dr. Porter said that is what would happen if I walked on it before it was ready."

"You are wicked! You are mad! Have you *really* thought what it will mean? All your life?" Christina was horrified.

"Yes, of course I've thought. I've had plenty of time to think, haven't I? And I think it's worth it, and you won't make me change my mind."

"Just so that you don't have to ride? Is it really as bad as that?"

"Hunting is, yes."

"I don't believe it. Not to have a stiff leg all your life. You'll be a cripple."

"Look, if I have to go hunting, I shall be worse than a cripple in a year or two. I shall be dead. I *do* hate it that much. You don't know how it feels, to be a passenger on a horse you can't stop, with Mark just ahead of you and your horse not intending to get behind and lose sight of its stablemate. And Mark—Mark being so mad—he will stop for nothing, and I have to follow whether I like it or not."

"Don't be so stupid. It's not like that," Christina said.

"It is for me. It will be all right for you. You're a girl. You'll be given Sweetbriar, and you can go through the gates and Dick will look after you, like he did this afternoon. But

Father is such a maniac—I cannot stand facing him night after night with all that claptrap, and him knowing I am afraid. He has never been afraid in his life; he does not know how it feels. And if I cannot ride he will wash his hands of me. I shall be left in peace. He will hate me, but that will make no difference."

"But it's only for a few years, till you're old enough to do as you please. And your leg will be for ever."

"I know. But I've made up my mind. In any case, Dr. Porter said he thought it was going to mend stiff. That's what he's been shaking his head about. He told me on no account to put it out of bed, to give it the best chance, and that's what gave me the idea. I'm only helping on a bit what's already happening."

"It is wicked, what you are doing," Christina said.

"It's my life. And you can't guess how I feel about hunting. I am a coward. I am terrified. And why should I be reminded what a coward I am four days a week for the next seven years? You just think about it—you don't know how I feel—" William's voice choked to a stop. Christina sat back on her heels and stared at him sternly. He looked very vulnerable, as he had looked the first time she had set eyes on him on the homemade stretcher, but the stubborn determination in his voice was unanswerable. He was, by his own admission, a little cowardly boy. And yet, Christina thought, she was shocked not by his cowardliness, but by the cold appalling courage with which he was working out what he thought was his salvation.

"You see," he went on, "I shall be able to fly with a stiff leg. It will just mean adjusting the rudder bar a bit . . . It will make no difference to what I really want to do."

"You are mad," Christina said. It was the only thing she could state with any certainty.

She did not know what to do. She sat by the hearth, feeling the warmth filtering through her flannel nightgown, looking doubtfully at William. She knew she ought to tell Mary what was happening; she wished Mary were there now. Wil-

liam seemed to have shrunk inside the blanket, his thin face
drawn with pain. His eyes glittered with the brandy.

"You're not going to tell anyone about this?" he said.

Christina did not answer. She was thinking, "I must. I
cannot let him do this."

"Are you?" William insisted.

"I—I don't know."

William leaned forward, his lips trembling. "If you tell anyone, if you *interfere*—"

"What?" Christina looked at him nervously. "It's not to be
unkind, William—don't you see? But what you're doing—"

"I have thought about it. I know what I'm doing. I promise
you, if you interfere, I—oh, I know!" His face cleared suddenly.
"I know what I shall do. If you tell Mary, or Mark, or Father,
I shall tell Father that Dick poaches in our covert. It is true,
I have seen him, and Dick knows that I know. And if you tell
anybody about me, I shall tell Father, and Dick will get a
flogging and be dismissed. Mark used the same threat over
you, not to tell about Treasure. Now it's my turn."

"You wouldn't!"

"I promise you I would. This means far more to me than
Dick's welfare."

"Oh, William, you are raving. Get back to bed. I will help
you. We'll talk about it in the morning."

"In the morning it will be the same."

"Oh, you stubborn beast! Come on, get up, while you still
can. If you faint here I shall *have* to call Mary."

Christina could not bear having to make a decision, with
William's feverish eyes fixed on her. The physical problem of
getting him back to bed was enough to occupy her. She got
up sternly.

"Come on. We can't talk all night. Get up, if you're so
determined to walk. I can't carry you."

She rated him, bearing his weight on her shoulder, terrified
he would not complete the journey. She could not understand
how he could voluntarily inflict such pain on himself, and still
call himself a coward. She thought, as the firelight flared, and

the grotesque shadows mimicked them on the wall, that his sense of values was as shattered as his knee. She got him to the end of the bed and he sat on it, and she pulled the covers down so that he could roll in. She had to lift the heavy plaster while he heaved himself up on his arms; he cried out, and she had to take no notice, and shove him into place. By the time she had got him covered up again, she was sweating and sick with his pain, and furiously angry with him for causing her such distress.

"See what you're doing to yourself!" she hissed at him, almost in tears. "It would serve you right if you never walk again, like your father!"

He lay back on the pillows, half-conscious, muttering something she could not catch. She sat by him in the glow of the firelight, till his whimpering breathing quieted, and his eyes closed. Once he twitched like a dreaming cat, and cried out, "Mr. Dermot!" Then he slept again.

Christina, exhausted, went back to bed.

William's Strange Ideas

"Have you ever heard of a Mr. Dermot?" Christina asked Dick.

"No, miss. Never."

"He must live near here, I think."

"He's not a hunting man then. Nor keeps horses, or I should know of him."

"He's a flying man."

"A flying man?" Dick laughed. "Why, miss, there's no such thing, only in America."

"Can I jump today?" Christina changed the subject.

"Yes, miss. If you're going out Boxing Day we'd best practice a few ditches."

"Mark says Mr. Lucas is bringing the hounds to Flambards for the Boxing Day meet."

"Yes, miss. They always meet here Boxing Day."

"If I ride Boxing Day then, you'll be with me?"

"Yes, miss."

"Who will take Mark's second horse? Isn't that generally your job?"

"Yes, miss. Mickey can take it. Or Harry."

"Do you think I shall ever need a second horse?"

"Why not, miss? I don't reckon you'll need me to look after you for long. They say your mother and Miss Grace used to stay out all day, and Mrs. Russell did, I know."

"Wouldn't you rather hunt properly, than be a second horseman?"

Dick looked puzzled. "Yes, of course. If I were Mr. Mark now, on Treasure . . ." His eyes gleamed for a moment. "Why, I—" He paused. "Well, I reckon I know when I'm well off. I get my sport out of being second horseman, in a way. It's a game of its own, you know, to follow a hunt and be at a check with the horse still fresh, cutting corners and trying to think one ahead of the fox, so's you can guess where they're going to end up. And be there, without having gone out of a trot." He added softly, "Mr. Mark should try it some time."

"I'll try to need you as long as possible." Christina said gravely. "So that you can hunt properly."

Dick grinned. "The way you're going on, miss, you won't need me more than a few times. Come on, if you want to try a jump. There's a drain at the bottom of the slope that will suit you nicely. Keep her steady, not too fast."

The boy in Dick restrained a whoop of exhilaration as the two horses broke into a canter. He rode beside Christina on Woodpigeon, matching Sweetbriar's pace, watching Christina very still and workmanlike in the saddle, her eyes shining with excitement as they approached the jump. The two horses lengthened their stride, shoulder to shoulder, and jumped the drain with a flourish of their tails. Christina sat back, and let Sweetbriar have her mouth.

"Splendid!" Dick shouted.

He grinned at her, and neither of them wanted to stop. It was too good, with the winter grass beneath and the horses with their ears raked forward, their gray manes flying. Dick stood up in his stirrups and Woodpigeon started to gallop, Sweetbriar beside him, and this time Christina was confident, utterly trusting in her own ability, and in the infallibility of Dick. She looked across at him and laughed. Now it was right to be galloping: a great joy surged through her. And all the while the glory of it filled her with this new and incomparable happiness, she was conscious right at the back of her mind of a pity for William, and a little bit of contempt.

Dick pulled up at the end of the big field, and Christina
was able to check Sweetbriar without any difficulty, dropping
back to a mild canter and milder trot without losing her dignity. She turned a glowing face to Dick.

"Oh, that was magnificent!"

They rode back through the woods, the two horses side by
side along the peaty ride, their hoofs not making a sound.
The trees closed around them, silent and bare, giving off scents
of fungus and damp and trodden earth that mingled with the
steamy fragrance of sweat on leather. Neither of them spoke.
Christina was conscious of a deep content, which words could
not improve, sharply conscious of every detail around her,
which seemed to shine out with an intensity to match her own
happiness. What Dick was thinking she could not tell, but
Christina was aware that her own feelings owed very much
to the presence of Dick, who had yet to offend her by any
word or action. He rode watching the path ahead, his face
composed, his eyes very blue, giving nothing away, under the
velvet peak of his cap. He was a perfect servant, Christina
thought, with a sudden, uneasy twist of her heart.

Christina liked hunting. From the first moment when, on
Boxing Day, Mr. Lucas rode up Flambards' drive with the
hounds in a rippling fluid wave about his horse's legs, she felt an
unaccountable excitement in the atmosphere. She had not expected to be impressed, but she was. She had expected to be
nervous and full of sympathy for the fox, but she found herself instead thrusting for her place with all the impatience of
her cousin, and her heart fields ahead with the running pack.
The ground was sodden with rain, the air mild. Dick took a
line of his own, and Sweetbriar galloped by his side, and when
there was a check Christina was always there, once ahead of
Mark. Mark noticed this with a dark, offended glance. When
Mark had ridden on, Christina noticed that Dick was smiling.

The first fox was killed after a run of six miles, with several
checks. Christina was glad not to see the final scuffle, which
occurred on the other side of a bank in a scrub of willow

osiers. She rode up in time to hear a thin animal scream cut short. The huntsman came out of the scrub on foot, holding some scraps of mangled meat, and Dick rode forward and said something to him. He grinned, and came across to Christina and she was duly blooded. She shut her eyes, felt the warm, stinking blood on her face, and thought—unaccountably —of William. Everyone was very kind to her, the smart ladies with impressively small waists smiling and nodding, and the gentlemen saying they remembered her mother. For the first time since she had come to Flambards, Christina was in contact with her neighbors, and she rode home with Dick full of warmth for the experience. A half day, Dick said, was enough for the first time out: she had seen good sport, and the hunts-

man had given her a paw. He tied the muddy little paw to her
saddle, and Christina remembered that it was an honor, a
trophy. It revolted her; it was so wet and defeated.

For the first time she ran into the house to find Uncle
Russell. He was dozing in his chair beside the fire, but when
she came in he jerked awake, and lay looking at her as she
stood in the doorway in her habit, the blood still on her face.
His black eyes took her in, slowly, inquiringly, and he smiled.

"Well?"

"Oh, it was lovely!" Christina said. "I had to come and tell
you. It was wonderful!"

His craggy old face was all split with pleasure. She had to
go and sit by him and tell him what had happened. He asked

where they found, and in what direction the fox went away, and what hounds did well, and held on to the line, but Christina did not know the names of the coverts and the fields, nor one hound from another. He prompted her, got exasperated, laughed, told her to open the bottle of port, and told her how he once hunted the same fox for fifteen miles in an hour and twenty minutes. Christina crouched by the fire, sleepy after the excitement, and thought, "I am away, committed. A hunting Russell." It had not taken long. When at last she got away from the old man, and trailed upstairs to her room, she felt she could not face William, and she washed and changed very slowly, looking at the blood on her face in the wardrobe mirror.

January came hard and sparkling. On the days when the ground was fit for hunting, Christina's heart bounded with excitement. She would jump out of bed and run to the window, and see the sun already thawing out the frozen ground; she would sing as she dressed and run downstairs two at a time. Mark would grin at her, and Uncle Russell started to talk about getting her a horse of her own. "Tell Fowler to come and see me," he said.

"A proper Russell," William would say to her when she went in to him in her riding clothes. He teased her, and she felt uncomfortable with him, embarrassed by liking hunting. Since she had found him walking across his bedroom, she had felt very confused by William; she could not understand him, yet in many ways he was far closer to her than Mark. She had not mentioned the incident to anyone, and believed that he had not attempted to do it again. But, whether by his own efforts or because of the original seriousness of his accident, his knee was locked when the plaster was removed, and Dr. Porter said there was nothing more he could do.

"You'd better start getting used to it," he told William. "You can go downstairs now. Get your muscles working again. Get some fresh air. And regret nothing. There are many people worse off than you."

William could no longer defer meeting his father again.

Christina believed that this ordeal was far worse to him than
the agony of sabotaging his knee. When he was dressed and
ready to go down for the first time, he stood, very silent and
pale, waiting for Mary, one hand holding the brass bedknob
and the other lifted to one of the flying machines, revolving
it gently on its white thread. Christina did not dare say a
word. When Mary came she followed them along the passage,
watching William's slow, stiff progress. Mary walked by his
side, but he did not need any support. He went down the
stairs, holding the banisters, a stair at a time, and Russell came
out into the hall and stood watching him. Christina looked
at her uncle, but saw no emotion in his face, no smile of
welcome, just a faint contempt. William finished the stairs
and halted at the bottom and looked at his father. Christina
hurried down and stood beside him, for moral, not physical
support.

"So, that makes two of us," Russell said.

"Yes, sir."

Christina was half shocked, half pleased, to sense a comple-
mentary contempt in William's voice.

"We'll see what you've learned," Russell said roughly.

He was in his worst mood, Christina could see, heavy with
drink and full of self-pity. William followed him into his lair,
where Mary had pulled up another chair by the fire. On a
table by Russell's chair was the pile of books so familiar to
Christina, and beside them, a cane. Christina was horrified
by the cane. She had not believed he could be so cruel. William sat down after his father was seated, and looked at the
cane, without any expression on his face. Christina, on edge,
could not bear to be a close witness to this inquisition, nor
could she bear to go away and not know what was happening.
She went to the far end of the room and got some writing
materials, to write to Aunt Grace. "Suppose," she thought, "I
describe exactly what is happening now? Aunt Grace will know
we are all mad in this house."

But Christina need not have worried. William knew the
answer to every question his father asked him, endlessly reel-

ing off the meaningless jargon from the breeding of Flambards' Huntress to the last sentence of Goodall's *Practice With Foxhounds*.

"At least," Russell said thickly, "you will know what we are talking about, even if it will never be your good fortune again to participate."

Christina bent her head over her paper. "Why," she thought, "he hates William . . . he hates him. . . ."

William came downstairs each night for dinner, and on hunting days, when the talk was all of the day's sport, he sat patiently, never saying a word. Only Christina tried to talk to him, to include him, but he made no effort to meet her, so that she gave up bothering.

William went his own way. Christina had to admit that he had gained by becoming crippled. Now that the damage was irrevocable, she sensed a tranquility in William that she was sure had not been there before. She had never known him in his hunting days, but she knew his feelings now well enough to guess what a hell his life must have been before the accident. As the weeks went by he gained strength, and went out walking, so that he became a familiar figure around the fields and woods with his awkward gait. There was nothing aimless about what he did. Christina, watching him trailing across the garden once, returning from one of his walks, was aware of a mystery about William. He was no nature lover, to walk for pleasure. He walked for a purpose.

When she questioned him, he said, "How else can I get about, until I am old enough to earn some money and buy a car? You don't think I want to stay in Flambards every day, do you?"

"You could drive the trap out."

"Oh, horses!" William was contemptuous.

Christina guessed that William did not want to involve anybody else. To take the trap would mean asking Fowler, and making his business public. William liked to go his own way, alone, independently.

When summer came, William was away more and more.

Russell did not bother to inquire after him. Mark was required to make up his education, which suffered in the winter, and spent every morning with Mr. Johnson, the tutor, groaning and swearing over grammar and mathematics. Christina joined him three mornings a week, and found herself enjoying the ordinariness of learning sums again, even with such a reluctant classmate as Mark. The tutor was a long-suffering young man who came from the vicarage. He was the vicar's son, prevented by ill health from taking any more arduous employment. Not that teaching Mark was any sinecure. He was surly and unwilling. Christina became used to the routine of the long, hot mornings in the study, with the bluebottles droning in the windows and the paper set before her with her own neat, round writing looking peculiarly satisfying. So normal, she used to think, when everything else at Flambards was so strange and disturbing. She got on well with the tutor, and he liked to have a serious, well-behaved pupil for a change. On the occasions when William decided to take lessons, Christina noticed that the young man treated him with a mixture of deference and exasperation. The feeling seemed to be mutual. The reason for it, Christina discovered, was William's fault.

"He has an exceptionally brilliant mathematical brain," the tutor said to her once. "He is now beyond my ability to teach, as far as mathematics is concerned."

Once the tutor said to William, "Do you get lessons from anyone else, besides me?"

William shook his head, and said, "No, sir," in such an innocent voice that Christina looked up sharply. She examined his expression, and did not believe him. But when she questioned William later he said, "Where else should I get lessons from, in this wilderness?"

"From Mr. Dermot, whoever he may be," Christina said.

William's eyes flared angrily.

"Mr. Dermot is dead," he said.

By late summer Russell had bought two new horses, one for

Christina and one for Mark. Christina was at first doubtful about her animal, having first loyalty to the gentle Sweetbriar, but when she had ridden him a few times, she had to admit that he was as Mark described him, "a little cracker." He was a cocky-looking bay, heavily built, with a banged tail and a small white star on his forehead. Although he was full of go, he was a lady's ride, in that he would stop when asked, which Christina already looked on as a prime virtue in a horse. His name was Drummer, and he had cost Russell two hundred pounds. Mark's horse, Cherry, was a big, ugly light bay mare with black points. She had big feet and an honest head and a reputation that brought her price up to two hundred and fifty. Russell had the new horses ridden out for his inspection up and down the drive. When he was satisfied, Christina and Mark rode them back to the stables, and the boys admired them, and they were given scrubbed out box stalls and summer sheets with Russell's initials in the corners.

Back in the kitchen, Mary said crossly, "New curtains for the dining room now, and it's another matter. Not to mention some new crockery, and a carpet in the study . . ."

Christina, her conscience pricking her, got a tin of polish from the cupboard and went around trying to make the house shine. When she pulled the curtains in the evenings, she saw what Mary meant when one of them came down in her hand, leaving the part with the rings on still hanging, shredded, from the rail.

The chestnuts started to turn yellow, their conkers ripening in the long golden afternoons.

"We should have tea on the lawn," Christina thought, but the lawn was a wilderness of seeding grass, full of bees and butterflies and the old pink roses, full-blown, scattering their petals into the richer pink of the willow herb that had grown, uninvited, on the terrace. The sun gilded the rambling house, and the grass beyond the railings where the hunters were turned out. Christina roamed, perfectly contented, thinking, "Soon I shall have been here a year." Battersea seemed very far away.

Soon the horses were taken up and shod, and the boys in the stables worked longer and longer hours, grooming and exercising, walking the summer fat off the horses. Hunting of fox cubs started, and Christina rode out with Mark. Dick held Drummer for her while she mounted. It was only seven-thirty, yet the horses were shining, and everything in place. Dick had grown taller. Looking down on him as he tightened Drummer's girths, Christina saw the sun-bleached hair lying pale against the brown of his neck. She thought, with an instinctive sympathy, "I must have Dick ride with me when hunting proper starts. I must not get good too quickly." She remembered the gleam in his eyes when he had said, "If I were on Treasure . . ." But now he just said, "That's it, miss," and stepped back, and she said, "Thank you," and rode away with Mark.

Dick hunted with her till Christmas, by which time it was evident that she needed no escort. Yet when Dick stopped coming, Christina missed his company far more than she had expected to. She missed his observations, and having someone to giggle with sometimes, and his way of making her feel that someone understood how she felt. Dick understood her, more than either of her cousins. "At least," Christina thought, trying to work out what it was, "we think the same way. We're not mad, like Mark and Will." And all the time there was this baffling thing that, although much less obtrusive then once it had been, still lay between them: so that Dick called her "miss" and never teased her as her cousins did, never called her a ninny or laughed out of place. As she grew older Christina became more conscious of this barrier; she resented it, but understood that it was a perfectly proper thing.

"Why is it?" William said, when she got involved with him once on the subject. "I don't see why."

"But of course," Christina said.

"We're all the same as each other, aren't we?" William said. "It's only luck what we get born into. Flambards, or Buckingham Palace, or a pig farm. It's only my luck that I don't have to work, and Dick's bad luck that he does have to. But we're just the same, as people."

Christina was completely out of her depth, trying to follow.

"We all have our place. You say it's just luck—"

"Well, it's not brain. It should be, but it isn't. It's pure luck, whether you are born a slave, or a slave driver."

Christina laughed. "You're talking pure rubbish. Who is a slave, for goodness' sake? Fowler? He loves working here. It's everything to him, all he wants."

"Yes, it is to Fowler. He doesn't want much, after all. But take Dick. Have you seen the way he looks, sometimes, when Mark shouts at him? He knows that he knows more than Mark, can ride as well as Mark, and get more out of a horse than Mark. But Mark will always be able to tell Dick what to do. Why is that fair?"

"If Dick doesn't like it, he can always leave, and get another job. I don't see anything unfair about it."

"It would be fair if Dick *could* leave and get another job. But if Dick wants another job he will have to get a good reference from Father or Mark. And if they don't choose to give him one, what can he do? Why do you say he's not a slave?"

"Because he gets paid, and he likes the work."

"Do you know how much he gets paid?"

"No."

"His wages are ten shillings a week. Out of that he pays rent and keeps his sick mother. The fact that he likes his work is the only bit of luck on his side, by my reckoning."

Christina was silent. She was amazed by William's argument, which sounded like something out of the newspapers. Although she had instinctively been irked by the convention that stopped Dick and herself being friends, it had never occurred to her that it was something to question. And, in spite of William, she still did not see how it could be changed.

"But people who employ servants look after them," she said. "I don't see how you can call servants slaves."

"Some employers look after their servants and some don't. I don't see how you can think that my father worries about his servants' welfare. On the other hand, someone like—" He hesitated, and continued, "Well, some of them do. It depends on their—" he groped for the right word—"humanity." He paused again, and added, "But why should it? People should earn their places, not be born into them."

"Oh!" said Christina, exasperated. "Someone has been giving you all these ideas. You are talking like a—what do they call them?—a Rad—Radical. You should stand for Parliament. If your father heard you talk like that, he would throw you out."

"He has, to all intents and purposes, hasn't he?" William said quietly. He was flushed with anger. "Oh, you!" he burst out petulantly. "You are just like the rest of them! I thought you were going to have more sense. They have got you thinking just the same way, as if hunting is all there is in life—"

"I like that!" Christina retorted. "It is you whose ideas are so funny! Where do you get them from, that's what I'd like to know? Where do you learn politics? Not from Mr. Johnson, that's certain. I suppose you get them from the same place as you get your mathematics?"

"It's no business of yours what I do, or what I think," William said furiously. A year after his accident, he had grown tall, and seemed much older, older than Mark at times. He was still very thin, his outgrown clothes stretched tight over his bones, so that his wrists showed, and his long, sensitive hands looked enormous. For all his walking, he never got brown like Mark and Dick, and his pallor was emphasized by the black hair that hung over his forehead and the dark, withdrawn eyes. It struck Christina afresh how apart he was, how little any of them knew him. Where did he go to? she wondered. Who fed his unusual intelligence? By comparison, Mark was as unsubtle as the most honest of their horses; he was completely single-minded, and lived only for fast, hard riding. Horses apart, he was lazy, rude, affable, and occasionally charming. At fifteen he was physically mature, handsome (Christina remembered Violet, with a little pang), and—Christina had to admit it—not very intelligent. Remembering Aunt Grace's prophecy concerning her marriage, Christina, as yet, had no feelings on the matter at all.

PART TWO: *1910*

Sweetbriar Turns a Somersault

Christina had a new habit made for her fifteenth birthday, the indefatigable Mary having let out Aunt Isabel's habit to its ultimate frayed dart during the last two winters. With some new stays to improve her waist, Christina turned herself around in front of her bedroom mirror with considerable satisfaction. Even if her stock of day dresses, supplied by Aunt Grace every spring and autumn, was not in the first flight of fashion, at least in her new habit she looked splendid, like a hard-riding débutante from the cream of the grass country. She lifted her chin, and pulled out some curls from under the brim of the new bowler to lie on her forehead. She had wanted to put her hair up, bundled at the back of her head so that the bowler would have to sit well forward at an angle Christina thought terribly dashing, but Mary was shocked at the suggestion, and would not hear of it.

"At your age, miss! Whatever next!"

Mark raised his eyebrows and whistled when he saw her.

"Who d'you think you are, then? Did you get Father to pay for that?"

"Yes. For my birthday."

"I didn't get anything when I was seventeen. Only a lecture about not getting girls into tr—about behavior, I mean." He grinned. "Perhaps I could get a new pair of boots out of him."

"You had new breeches for the point-to-point run."

Mark scowled. "I'd rather have won in my old ones than lost in the new ones."

"Next year," Christina said.

In the spring Mark had ridden Treasure in the hunt races, but because of their joint inexperience, they had only come in fourth. Mark had been furious. His own enthusiasm had inflamed the already excitable Treasure, so that he had made several bad mistakes, but the horse was considered to have a big future, and already Mark was counting the days to the next race. Christina thought, secretly, that if Dick could have ridden Treasure, the horse would have won, for Dick had had a remarkably calming effect on Treasure during the three years he had cared for him.

Dick noticed her new habit too; she could tell by the way his eyes carefully did not look, after the first flare of surprise.

She laughed and said, "Don't you think I look smart, Dick? I'm as smart as Drummer now."

"Why, yes, miss. You're a right pair." He smiled, flushing slightly. He did not chat any more—as he once had when they had ridden through the fields together. Christina had noticed, gradually, that he no longer started conversations, nor passed remarks, but only replied to her own observations. He had withdrawn, and she knew it was because of the convention that she had discussed with William. He treated her with more respect. A small part of Christina was flattered by this, but a larger, more logical part was grieved. She had wanted Dick to go on being a friend, as he had been when he had taught her to ride, but now the barrier between them was preventing it. What William had said, although she had laughed at him, had stuck in her mind, but Christina saw no way of bridging this gulf. She also felt that Dick was more anxious to keep it than she was herself, and she had a feeling that he wanted it in some way as a protection for himself, but as a protection from what, she had no idea. When she was older she realized what it was, but when she was fifteen she had only vague feelings which she could never pin down, nor analyze. She always admired William for the way he was able to explain everything with his mathematician's logic, but she did not think that even William could explain what some of her feelings meant, nor even what they were. She thought that Aunt Grace would have been more helpful, with her brisk, "It's your age."

Out hunting, she had no worries. Her horses were superb, and she was afraid of nothing. When people told her she was "fearless," she sometimes wondered if it was because she had no imagination, as William had told her. But on Sweetbriar and Drummer she never had cause to be afraid; she was never foolhardy, like Mark, and would turn away from a fence if she decided that it was too big for her. If Mark had to do this it sent him into a frenzy, but Christina kept her head, having learned patience the hard way. Although she took several falls, she was never hurt. In the evenings, at dinner, she would discuss the day's sport with her uncle and Mark—and now she

knew whether it was Plowman or Rockwood who first owned
the line, and Partridge who got into trouble over a hare—
and Russell's eyes would flash over his wineglass. William
would sit silently, in a world of his own. In spite of his father's
scorn, he never touched any drink but water. Christina, accustomed now to the Russell ways, stopped worrying about
William.

Christina, like Mark, regretted the all too hasty passing of
the winter days. By February one could almost count off the
remaining hunting days on one's fingers. After a period of
hard frost which canceled three days' hunting, she rode with
Mark to a meet at the Ferrers Arms with the feeling that
these next few weeks must make up for the week they had
just missed and all the weeks to come.

"Summer's awful," Mark agreed. "After the point-to-point—
nothing. Father thinks I ought to go up to Oxford. Can you
imagine it?"

"No," Christina said. "William ought to," she added.

"He never said anything about William going. He's welcome to it, I say."

It was a good day, cold and clear. Christina was on Drummer, and Mark on Treasure, and Dick was bringing on Woodpigeon and Sweetbriar as second horses. Drummer was on his
toes. "He's as bad as Treasure," Christina said.

"Good as, you mean," Mark said.

Mr. Lucas' hounds (many of them veterans bred by Russell
when he owned them) were lean and fast. "They would never
win prizes for looks," Russell had said often enough, "but
they know their job." They drew a covert called Four Ashes,
and were away in minutes, and Christina knew, with one of
her "feelings," that it was going to be a good day. The ground
was firm, not too sticky, and the turned plow gleamed where
the big horses had patiently worked over it. The farmer had
left a wide edge of grass and Drummer went down it like an
arrow from a bow, clods flying from his hoofs. All the rest
of the field had gone away on the other side, but Christina,
rather than wait in the hustle for the gate out of the wood,

had decided to go around. If the fox ran to the left up to Stag's Bushes, as he usually did, she would be right up with hounds on the other side. She knew this wood well. She pulled at Drummer to steady him, and he went over the timber at the bottom of the field as neatly as a cat. Here they could cross the spur of woodland unimpeded. The peaty ride was their own. Bending down to miss the branches, Christina smelled the leather and the sweat and the flying peat; Drummer was all lathery with excitement, taut and sweet beneath her. She steadied him again, because of the branches, and she thought of the hounds running ahead and laughed out loud. Sometimes when she felt like this she laughed, but half of her wanted to cry. The excitement went through her like a current.

The jump out of the wood was narrow, three plain bars covered with lichen, and high. It needed careful judgment, and she shut her lips tight as she rode at it, concentrating hard. Drummer pulled and raked out, too keen, but she had time to steady him; he saw the bars in plenty of time, and Christina got him just right, so that even as he took off she knew it was all right. It was beautiful, and clever, and filled her with wonderful satisfaction. There was no one to see, but she thought, "If nothing more happens today, it has been worth it."

But the glory of the day had barely started. The fox had turned left, as Christina had hoped, and out of the wood she found only Mr. Lucas and his huntsman ahead of her, and the best stretch of grass in the country under her heels. Hounds were running in a bunch, fast, along the bottom of the big sloping valley. For a moment she held Drummer, looking down on the two red coats and the rippling hounds, then the little bay leaped forward and started to gallop down the hill in pursuit. She only had to sit, hands still, and feel the cold air splintering past her face.

At the end of the valley there was a brief check which enabled the strung-out field to catch up, then they were away again across a field of kale. Christina found Mark, and they had time to grin at each other as they jumped a low hedge side by side into a lane. Mark, in his usual fashion, took

Treasure out over a blind bank which Christina would not consider; she did not see him again until the next check on the edge of a piece of woodland, by which time the horses were tiring, and a large part of the field had disappeared. Mark rode up in a flurry of mud and said, "If only that damned Dick would arrive with Woodpigeon!"

Christina, getting her breath, said, "If anyone can get them here, Dick will."

Treasure was black with sweat. Drummer's sides heaved. Christina would have dismounted, but was afraid the hounds might go away again at any minute and leave her stranded.

"Perhaps if he goes out on the Fallowfield side we'll meet Dick on the road."

"Listen!"

Somewhere in the wood a hound was owning the line again. A cold breeze rattled the branches. Christina was anxious, wanting to go, but knowing Drummer was getting tired.

"They'll go out on the far corner," Mark said. "Come on."

"Yes, listen! They're away—"

"And up toward the road too."

Treasure and Drummer, hearing hounds, broke into a trot. Mark went ahead, but Christina nursed Drummer, holding him. They went around the bottom of the wood and saw Mr. Lucas going up the hill the other side, over rough pasture, hounds strung out over fifty yards ahead of him. Mark put Treasure into a canter again, but the going was heavy, and

Christina knew she ought to pull Drummer out. She looked across toward the road, and to her delight saw Dick coming through the gate at the top with Woodpigeon and Sweetbriar. Mark saw him at the same time, and altered course.

Christina started to canter for the gate. Dick had dismounted and as Mark rode up, instead of changing horses immediately, Dick said something to him, and they seemed to be having an argument. Christina, still some way behind, had guessed that something was wrong, because Dick had been riding Sweetbriar, and the cross-saddle was still on her. Usually he rode Woodpigeon, and led Sweetbriar, because Sweetbriar had the sidesaddle. Christina eased the laboring Drummer. She saw Mark slip down from Treasure, throw the reins to Dick, and jump up onto Sweetbriar.

"Whatever—" Christina was filled with indignation. "That's my horse! Mark!" she shouted. "Mark!"

But as she rode up to Dick, Mark was already away, turning in his saddle to shout something which Christina could not catch. Christina's eyes blazed.

"What's he doing? Dick, why did he take Sweetbriar?"

"I told him, miss, Woodpigeon's gone lame. So he took Sweetbriar. I couldn't stop him."

Dick was as angry as Christina.

"Oh, the beast! The beast!" Christina could have wept with rage. "And hark at them, Dick! Hark at them!"

Hounds had doubled back. They had crossed the lane and were running back on the other side, throwing their tongues with an abandon that set all the horses jigging, even the weary Drummer. Mr. Lucas and his huntsman were lost somewhere between the banks of the lane, and the only horseman in sight was Mark, coming down on the far side at a flat gallop. He was standing in his stirrups and quite oblivious of anything but the flying pack in front of him. With his fresh horse Christina knew just how he was feeling; a great sob of rage burst out of her.

"The beast! Oh, Dick, how could he?"

But she knew only too well how he could. She wondered,

if she had been Mark, if she could have resisted the tempta-
tion herself. She watched Sweetbriar's flying white tail, and
the big hedge that stood in her way at the bottom of the hill.
Mark was going at it as he did with Treasure, fast, his hands
up on the mare's neck. Christina, knowing Sweetbriar, frowned
and said to Dick, "Oh, the idiot! She'll go right through it."

But, watching him, Christina could feel Sweetbriar's long
stride, see the hedge as Mark saw it: a trifling obstacle between
him and that galloping pack whose wild music was filling the
valley. Seeing the hedge in cold blood, from up the hill, Christina shivered, and said, "Oh, Dick, the mare!"

Even as Sweetbriar rose at it, Christina knew that she was watching disaster. She saw the gallant attempt at a take-off from a ditch lip of brimming mud, heard the crack of the rails as the mare hit them with her forelegs, then the cartwheel arc of her iron shoes as she catapulted out of sight through the crackling brushwood. Christina looked at Dick. Even then, it was the mare's plight she was thinking of, not Mark's. Her own excitement was quenched; hounds were already out of sight in the woodlands along the bottom of the valley, and she felt cold at the sight of the accident.

"I reckon the mare'll be no better for that," Dick said shortly.

He mounted Treasure, and pulled the lame Woodpigeon up beside him. "We'd best go and see."

They went out of the gate and rode down the paved lane at a trot. Below the hedge where Sweetbriar had foundered there was a gate into the field. Christina opened it from Drummer, held it for Dick, then wheeled around and cantered ahead. Sweetbriar was lying where she had fallen, propped up on her forelegs half in and half out of the ditch, her eyes very wild, her flanks heaving. Mark was staggering out of the ditch beside her, his hands up to his face, not looking as if he knew quite where he was going. The sight of him on his feet, conscious, switched Christina's whole attention to the mare; for Mark her fear dissolved into a furious contempt.

"What have you done to her?" she shouted at him angrily. "You've half killed her!"

She slid off Drummer and ran toward Sweetbriar. But Dick came alongside and shouted, "Leave her to me! You hold the horses." He jumped off Treasure, and threw Christina the reins, so that she was suddenly entangled with the reins of three wheeling horses. She tried to calm them and watch Dick at the same time, trembling with indignation. Dick was standing by Sweetbriar's head, talking to her, encouraging her to get out of the ditch. She quietened with Dick by her, but her eyes were black with pain. Christina watched in an agony of fear for the mare.

"What's wrong? What's the matter with her, Dick?"

"Come on, old lady . . . come up out of there, my old dear. You'll be better when you're four-square, my old horse. . . ." With Dick coaxing her, Sweetbriar scrabbled again and clawed with her trembling legs at the sliding earth.

With a rush the mare came up on the the grass, but her legs were shaking so that she almost keeled over. Dick put his shoulder to hers and held her, talking to her all the while. Mark came up to Christina and Christina took her eyes off Sweetbriar for a moment to look at him. His face was covered with mud and his nose was pouring blood, which was splattering his white collar and disappearing into the scarlet of his jacket.

"Look what you've done to the mare!" Christina raged at him. "You were mad to put her at that!"

"Look whad she's dod to be!" Mark muttered. "Fool horse . . . Have you god something to mob it with? I—ugh . . ."

"You ought to lie down," Christina said coldly. She turned

back to look at Sweetbriar, and saw that she was steady now, her head drooping, one foreleg pointed out. Dick was feeling her shoulders and ribs, taking off her saddle.

"What's wrong with her?"

"I'm not sure, miss. I think it's her shoulder—possibly a rib cracked. She took the fall on her near shoulder, I think. Her leg, you see . . ." He stood back, and looked at her thoughtfully.

"Will she be all right?"

"I can't tell, miss. She'll need a vet."

"What can we do with her now, though?"

"We'll have to see if she can get as far as the farm." He nodded down the hill. "Then get the vet up. Let's see if you can walk, old lady. Come on, my old girl. Try your old bones out. . . ."

He coaxed Sweetbriar forward and she took a few paces stumbling on her near fore, trembling.

"She'll get there, I think, miss. If I take my time."

"If we take the other horses home I can send Fowler out to help you," Christina said. "And call the vet. Would that be best?"

"Yes, miss. You go on now. It's doing those horses no good standing about. I'll see to the mare all right."

Christina looked coldly at Mark.

"Here, take Treasure. And you can jolly well lead Woodpigeon too. He's your horse."

Mark took Treasure's reins, and Christina, taking another look at him, relented a little. "Here, take my handkerchief. It's not very big though. You do look queer."

Mark's dark eyes looked balefully out of the mud and gore. He gathered up Treasure's reins and pulled himself up into the saddle with a groan. Christina maliciously handed him Woodpigeon's reins and said, "Take your horse. All this is your own fault entirely so you can't complain. It was a dirty trick to play on me. If I'd done the same to you, you wouldn't have been very pleased. Apart from what you've done to the mare—"

"Nag, nag, nag," said Mark.

Christina waited for Dick to come and give her a boost on Drummer. When she was settled, she said, "I'll be as quick as I can and send you some help."

"Thank you, miss." He hesitated, then said awkwardly, "If I'm held up here with the mare, late tonight, I mean, could you tell Violet what's happened? So my mother knows?"

"Violet?"

"My sister."

"Oh, yes. Of course."

"Thank you, miss."

Christina put Drummer into a trot to catch up with Mark. On top of everything that had just happened, she found herself astonished to know that Violet was Dick's sister.

She said to Mark, "Did you know Violet was Dick's sister?"

Mark looked at her as if she were mad. "I wouldn't care at the moment if she was his mother-in-law," he said. "What are you talking about?"

"Dick's just said would I tell his sister, if he's held up— meaning Violet. I never knew they were brother and sister."

"I don't see that it matters at all," Mark said. With two horses to cope with, and one hand still mopping at his nose, he looked furious. "That blasted mare of yours never even took off. Straight through it she went. I reckon she's broken my nose. Put her great hoof right in my face. I've never known a horse so clumsy."

"You're lucky she didn't break your skull!" Christina said furiously. "Riding at a place like that! The take-off was a sea of mud—what did you expect her to do but go right through it? Treasure would have done just the same. It's imbecile the way you ride. I wonder you weren't killed long ago. And now poor Sweetbriar—because of you . . ."

"Whom are you telling how to ride?" Mark said, equally furiously. "The mare's past it, that's her trouble. She's not worth keeping if that shoulder's going to be troublesome."

"What do you mean, not worth keeping? She carries me like a bird. I wouldn't change her for all the Treasures in England.

She's got manners, at least. Which is more than you can say of any horse you've ridden for a bit. Look at Treasure now, for instance!"

Treasure was jogging along crabwise, pushing his quarters into the subdued Woodpigeon. Mark gave him an angry chuck on the mouth.

"What was that fool Dick thinking of to bring me a lame horse anyway? He's to blame for all this. Woodpigeon wouldn't have blundered."

"You don't suppose Woodpigeon was lame when he set out, do you?" Christina said scathingly. "Dick's not a soothsayer, to guess the horse is going to go lame, is he? Probably something to do with the way you rode him last Saturday."

As they bickered it started to rain. Mark huddled down in his saddle. They had about eight miles to go, and as the roads slowly slipped away beneath the ringing hoofs Christina mellowed toward Mark and felt almost sorry for him. She had never known him so subdued and dejected. Then she thought of Sweetbriar, and Dick benighted in some dirty farm stable trying to make her comfortable, and she hardened again and set her lips, pressing Drummer into a trot.

When they got home Mark went indoors and she took the three horses around to the stables. She had rarely led one horse, let alone two before, and felt very competent as she clattered into the stableyard. "Just like Dick," she thought. Fowler came running out in alarm at the sight of her, and she explained to him what had happened, while he stood pursing his lips and shaking his head.

"I'll go myself, at once. Dick will have his hands full. I know the place you mean."

"And perhaps someone had better go for Dr. Porter. Mark thinks his nose is broken."

"Dear me, dear me." Fowler clicked his tongue, full of concern. "Harry will go, this instant. Leave it to me, miss. I'll see to it. You go up to the house now, and get yourself dry. I'll go straight out to Dick, so don't you worry."

The boys took the horses. Christina looked into the stables

and saw the glow of the lamps, the golden beds of straw, the
boys, one to a horse, rubbing them down, hissing through
their lips. It was warm and sweet-smelling, shining, the horses
mellowed by lamplight. Christina was struck by the picture;
the kindliness of it warmed her, and she ran back up to the
house to get some comfort herself. Her hair was heavy with
rain.

Mark was washing in the kitchen, as he usually did, but
this time with much moaning and groaning. With the mud
removed, his face was badly cut and swollen. Mary said, "You
must bathe that nose with cold water to get it down to size.
Fetch a cloth, Violet, and a bowl." Violet did as she was
told. Christina, drying herself by the fire, looked up through
the tangled curtain of her hair and saw Violet take the things
to Mark, and stand by him with a towel. Her face—and now
Christina saw the family likeness to Dick in it—seemed to
shine with sympathy; her big green eyes were filled with a
tenderness that shocked Christina. "Why, she—she—" Christina's mind struggled with a conception completely new to her.
She remembered Violet saying that Mark was handsome, but
it had never occurred to her that Violet could—could—Christina could not even acknowledge that there was a name for
Violet's feelings, so transparently evident as she stood over
Mark. She was suddenly quite furious, crouched there beside
the fire. She threw her hair back and stood up quickly.

"Violet, take some hot water up to my room." She spoke
with a sharpness that made Violet jump.

"Yes, miss."

Christina went upstairs feeling utterly confused. "Why did
I speak like that?" she wondered. "I must be tired." But she
knew she was jealous, and she could not understand why.
Jealous of whom, she wondered, for how could anyone be
jealous of Violet? Christina did not know. She felt angry and
upset, and all for no reason that she understood. She pulled
off her jacket.

"It must be my stays," she thought. It was certainly bliss
to undo them. Christina knew how well a small waist looked

with a good riding habit, and had gradually been making hers smaller and smaller. "Perhaps it is not very wise," she thought. When Violet came in she gave her Dick's message, and Violet said, "Thank you, miss," and withdrew very quickly—to get back to Mark, Christina thought.

"Oh!" Christina was exasperated. She changed into her prettiest dress and tied her hair back with a black ribbon. "I shall put it up next season. I don't care what Mary says," she thought.

When dinner was served, William came in rather late. Christina could tell by the color on his cheeks and his damp hair that he had been out, but Russell made no inquiries. He scarcely glanced at him, as he was giving his full attention to Mark's description of Sweetbriar's "idiocy." William looked at Mark, and a glint of amusement came into his face.

"Had a good day?" he said pointedly.

Mark's half-closed eyes darted him a murderous glance. Mary brought in some more gravy and said, "Dr. Porter's called, sir. Shall I tell him to wait?"

"Send him in. He can have a drink with us," Russell said.

Dr. Porter joined them, and drank several glasses of wine while they finished their dinner. To Christina it seemed a very long time since her first night at Flambards, when Dr. Porter had last joined them for dinner. She remembered William on the stretcher—the only time she had ever seen him in hunting clothes—and Mark helping get the supper—the only time he had ever done so. After three glasses of port she could hardly remember the time before Flambards—Aunt Grace and Battersea.

"Where have you been?" she asked William when they left the table.

He grinned at her. He was not little any more, but taller than Christina by a head.

"Nowhere."

"You were all wet."

"The roof must leak."

"Oh, you tell such lies!" Christina said. She went slowly up to her room. The rain was pattering steadily against the window and sliding off the ivy in drips from leaf to leaf. Christina pressed her nose against the glass, looked into the darkness, and thought of Dick still working. And Violet going home through the rain, warm with love for Mark.

Mr. Dermot

"How is Sweetbriar, Dick?"

Christina looked at the mare sadly. She had missed her the last month, and now the hunting season was all but over. Sweetbriar only went walking, led by Dick from Woodpigeon, and even when she walked she was stiff and slow.

"It's a long job, miss. She's getting on for twenty, you know. I doubt if you'll be hunting her again."

"Oh, Dick! Do you mean it? Is it as bad as that?"

"Fox-cub hunting perhaps. I can't see her ever being the same again, though."

Dick was putting the mare's night rugs on. Now that the evenings were lighter Christina came down to the stables sometimes, after hunting, to see that the horses were all right. She liked the stables, and the orderliness there.

"But if she's turned out for the summer, surely she'll be all right next season?"

"I doubt it, miss." Dick was in his shirt sleeves. He fastened the roller, and Christina, who had been rubbing Sweetbriar's pink velvet nose, buckled the breast strap for him. She sighed. It was almost dinnertime. She walked back up to the house and went to see if Mary had the table ready. It was scarcely dark; the fire looked pale in the hearth, and the big chestnuts outside the windows were covered with buds.

At dinner, Russell inquired after Sweetbriar.

Mark said, "The rate she's going on, she's not worth keeping."

"Whatever do you mean?" said Christina.

"She won't hunt again, so what good is she?" Mark said.

"At that age, a fall like that often finishes a good hunter," Russell said.

"If she goes I'd like to make an offer for that chestnut of Thornton's," Mark said. "You remember the one, Father. Eight-year-old, up to weight. By Willow Bough."

"Sweetbriar is my horse," Christina pointed out. "If she goes—" She gave Mark a hard look. Little by little Mark was taking over his father's role, making decisions, telling Fowler what he wanted without recourse to Russell.

Mark gave her a mocking grin. "You would like Thornton's chestnut."

"I wouldn't," Christina said. "Not like Sweetbriar. Anyway—" another thought struck her— "where does Sweetbriar go to, if she goes?"

"The kennels," Russell said.

Christina did not understand. Russell picked another slice of mutton off the meat dish with his fork and put it straight into his mouth. "Tell Dick to ride her over there tomorrow then, Mark, if it's as you say."

"Why the kennels?" Christina asked.

William joined in the conversation for the first time. "The dogs eat her," he explained. "It's the customary way of showing gratitude to an old hunter, to feed it to the dogs."

"Hounds," said Mark.

Christina dropped her knife and fork. "Feed it? You mean—" She could not finish her sentence. She started at Mark, and then her uncle. Russell laughed.

"What's the matter, child? Hounds have got to eat, haven't they? What's more natural?"

"But not Sweetbriar!"

"She's run her course. There's no good in feeding a useless horse, girl."

"But—"

Christina was too upset to finish her dinner. She tried not to cry in front of her cousins, but she was filled with a surge of grief. Every day she had been to see Sweetbriar, taking her sugar or a crust of bread, and every day she had known that there would never be another horse for her quite like Sweetbriar, who had taught her to ride. There were no tricks in Sweetbriar. She was utterly good-natured and trusting. If Dick rode her to the kennels, she would trust Dick right up to the moment he gave her a last caress. And then, to reward her with a—

Christina choked.

"Oh, really, Christina. Don't be such a fool." Mark looked completely confounded.

William gave her a troubled look, and said nothing; Russell just laughed. Christina pushed back her chair and ran out of the room. She went out of the front door and stood for a moment looking out across the park. It was a warm evening, the dusk filled with smells of earth and the shiverings and rustlings of country things. Christina felt wild, stifled. "They are going to kill her," she thought. And it was spring starting, the chestnut buds bulbous and furry, a new moon low in the sky, bright like a new horseshoe. "She has done her best all her life, and now they feed her to the hounds." Horses were so simple and willing and trusting. "She tried for Mark, although he was so mad. She didn't refuse. She tried. And look where it has got her." Christina could not bear to go back to the men. It was they who were the animals, she thought. She picked up her skirts and ran down the path. The stables were in darkness, the high windows full of pale stars.

"Sweetbriar!"

The darkness was filled with the soft munching of feeding horses, the hollow clonk of a hoof on straw-covered tiles. Sweetbriar let out a surprised whinny, deep in her throat, and pushed her gentle muzzle at Christina's hand. It was too much for Christina. She buried her face against the mare's mane and cried.

Christina's crying was noisy and uncontrolled. There was

no one to hear her, save the sympathetic horses, who munched on. Even Sweetbriar. She did not hear the cautious scrape of boots on tiles.

"Christina!"

She jumped around, startled out of her wits. It was Dick who stood there. Her eyes accustomed to the dark, Christina saw his familiar shape outlined, one hand on Sweetbriar's rump. After his first exclamation he said nothing. Christina could not see his expression; a fresh sob hiccuped involuntarily from her lips, and Dick came up to her. Christina said, "Oh, Dick, they—they—" but another sob stopped her, and it seemed quite natural then to cry with her face buried in Dick's rough jacket instead of into Sweetbriar's mane, and with his arms folded around her, very firm and comforting.

"Christina—miss—don't." Dick's voice was frightened, and soft.

But Christina could not stop. The feel of Dick's arms, and the comfort of his warmth and strength, the feeling of his gentleness, so that he held her and spoke to her as if she were a fractious, upset pony, went through her with such joy that she forgot what she was crying for, and only wanted to go on feeling loved and protected. She could never remember having had someone's breast to cry on, and someone to hold her. The sweetness of it made her tremble. Dick stroked her hair with his gentle hands and spoke softly, until she realized that he, too, was trembling. A small, instinctive doubt touched her, and Dick at the same moment withdrew slightly.

"Please, Christina . . . I—please go home."

The words were blunt, yet Christina by instinct knew why he said it, and that it was right. It was as if she understood everything at that moment, without having to try to understand. Everything was completely strange, and completely right. Dick followed her to the door and bolted it behind him, and they walked up the drive to the house, holding hands. Christina knew that it would not be right to talk about Sweetbriar; in fact she had almost forgotten Sweetbriar. She was very conscious of the touch of summer in the dusk, the smell of the earth, and the infinite beauty of the skyful of stars above the canopies of the chestnut trees. There was no sense of anything out of place, even when they reached the front door of Flambards and Dick leaned down and kissed her cheek. It was a gentle kiss, for a fractious pony, Christina thought. Dick smelled of hay and leather and sweat.

"It will be all right," he said. "Don't cry again."

But when she went indoors, Christina did not know what she should be crying for, Sweetbriar or Dick.

Christina woke very early, when it was still dark. She had slept fitfully, with fantastic dreams chasing through her head, which she could not remember when she woke. In the dawn, cold and clear, she remembered that Sweetbriar was going to be shot. The thought made her very angry. She also remembered that Dick had kissed her, and this thought shocked her. Yet she could not recall feeling shocked when he did it. "But he's only a servant," she thought. "I must have been mad." But even telling herself that, she could not wish it had not happened. It was as if she was shocked now because she thought she ought to be, more than because she really was.

She felt very worried. She turned her thoughts back to Sweetbriar. "I cannot let it happen," she thought. She got out of bed, pulled on her bathrobe and went out into the passage.

William was asleep, half-buried under the blankets, only one lock of black hair showing.

"William!"

He pushed his head out, astonished.

"What's wrong? What's the matter?"

"Listen, I must talk to you. You must help me."

"Help you? Whatever—?"

He rolled over and heaved himself up on his elbows.

"You heard what they said at dinner last night—they're going to have Sweetbriar shot this morning. What can I do?"

Christina sat on the bed, huddled up against the cold. "You are brainy. Can't you think of something? You must see, I can't just let them do such a brutal thing."

William groaned. "What can I do, for heaven's sake? They're like that; brutal is the word for it. But you won't get them to see it."

"Can't we take her away somewhere—hide her, or something? Surely we can? But I can't do anything on my own. If you were to help . . ."

William groaned again.

Christina said, "I've never asked you for anything before. I don't make a habit of it. And I helped you—I never told on you, about your leg, did I? I'm only asking you for a clever idea—it's not much, surely?"

"Oh, all right. I'm sorry. It's just that—oh—you know them by now, don't you? I don't know why you were so surprised last night. It shows there's hope for you yet, Christina. You're not too far gone on being a hard woman to hounds, if you can still see they're brutal and stupid."

"Oh." Christina did not dare answer back. William had turned the tables on her, but sounded as if he might be more disposed to help. He sat up in bed, pulling the blankets up to his chin.

Christina said, "The only thing I can think of is, when Dick rides her over to the kennels, to meet him on the way and say Uncle has changed his mind. Then if I could say I would lead her home, Dick would go back—"

"Not very bright," William said. "Then everyone in the stables would know she hadn't gone, and Mark would be bound to find out in no time. The only thing is to pretend to everyone that she really went to the kennels, so that everyone thinks she's dead and gone. But really she isn't. The only way you could do that would be through Dick."

"How do you mean?"

"He would have to take her out of the stables and go back again afterwards and say he had left her at the kennels. So that everyone would take it for granted the deed was done. But you would have to meet him on the way, and take Sweetbriar over, and hide her away where no one would see her. Very difficult."

"Possible?"

"It would be if Dick would agree. And if you could find a place to hide her—out of the county, it would have to be, to be safe. And if, afterwards, Mark did not think to check up with Mr. Lucas, or say something to him like, 'I hope your dogs enjoyed their Sweetbiar joints.' And Mr. Lucas would say, 'What Sweetbriar joints, my dear boy?' Then you would be in trouble."

"Well, Mark doesn't often talk to Mr. Lucas. I think the risk is not very great there."

"And all the arrangements about such menial tasks would be left to Dick and Fowler. Mark won't bother. So if we enlist Dick, and he covers up all right, it should work."

"After all, it's no crime we're planning," Christina said. "If it were found out, what have we done? Only done the hounds out of some food."

"Well . . ." William gave her a dubious, slightly amused look out of the corner of his eye.

"What about finding somewhere to take her, though? That's the hardest thing."

"I might be able to help you there. If everything else was arranged, I think I could manage that bit."

"Really?" For the first time, a light of optimism came into Christina's eyes. "If you could, most of the difficulties are solved."

"It really depends on Dick."

"We'll have to see him before he gets to the stables."

"That will be in about a quarter of an hour," William said, looking at the clock by his bed. "It's getting on for six now."

"Oh, dear! What shall we do? Waylay him? Will you come too? Please, William! Oh, William, please help. I can't bear for her to be killed. It must work!"

William sighed. "All right. We'd better buck up then. Get dressed and I'll see you in a minute."

In five minutes they were letting themselves out of the house into a misty, cold morning.

"Which way does Dick come?" Christina asked.

"Up the drive. From the village. We could walk down and meet him."

Christina felt cold and anxious and, now, very nervous about meeting Dick. "You think it will work?"

"It depends on Dick."

Strange, Christina thought, that Dick walked up the drive every morning at six o'clock while she was still in bed and asleep. Last night now seemed very unreal. And yet, when she saw Dick approaching, she remembered the close smell of him and the feel of his arms. A deep flush came into her cheeks. When he came up, she saw that his cheeks were crimson too; he was looking surprised and ashamed and questioning all together, and very vulnerable, Christina thought. Afraid. She could not say anything.

If William noticed their deep embarrassment, he did not comment on it. He said, "Dick, we wanted to talk to you. About Sweetbriar."

He told him what was proposed for Sweetbriar, which did not surprise Dick, and what they had in mind to save her life. "It's up to you really," William said. "If you are prepared to do it, we will do the rest. Meet you, and take her away. I promise you she won't be found afterward, so don't worry about that."

Dick did not say anything at once. He looked at Christina, then at his toe, tracing a pattern in the gravel. The flush had died out of his cheek; it was smooth and brown, freshly shaven. Christina remembered the roughness of it last night.

"Oh, please, Dick," she said. She looked up at him and met his eye, and saw at once that he would do anything she asked him.

"Very well," he said.

William said, rather anxiously, "You are sure?"

Dick nodded. "Yes, sir."

"We'll wait for you in the wood up by Lucas' then."

It was easier than Christina expected. Knowing the routine of the stables, she knew what time Dick would come. Dressed in her brown tweed walking clothes and her thick walking boots she went up to the wood with William. William, for all his stiff leg, walked easily, and Christina, so used to Mark's company outside the house, was aware of an unexpected pleasure in being with William. He was undemanding, amusing; the great nervous frustrations that he had suffered when Christina had first got to know him seemed to have been banished. Since he no longer hunted, he was no longer persecuted by his father, but ignored. Christina had to admit that the plan had worked.

When she remarked on this, William said fervently, "Oh, yes! I was right, wasn't I? I'd still be hunting, but for this." He tapped his leg affectionately. "Killed by now, for sure," he added cheerfully. "The whole business was the best thing in the world to have happened to me."

"Even walking around the room with your bones grating together?" Christina asked.

"Worth it," William said happily.

"I do believe Mark has made more fuss over his nose than you ever made over your knee."

"Well, it's spoiled his beauty rather," William pointed out.

"Yes, a bit. But Mark's not vain."

"He likes seeing the girls' eyelashes flutter. I don't think he's very pleased."

"Oh, he's still handsome enough," Christina said, thinking of Violet. It was odd, but to think of Mark being interested in other girls, and other girls being interested in Mark, annoyed her. She had the same twinge of exasperation as she had experienced over Violet. She could not understand why.

As they walked into the stillness of the big covert half a mile from Lucas', squelching up the soft, hoof-churned ride, Christina suddenly thought of something terribly important. She stopped and faced William.

"Where are we taking Sweetbriar to, anyway? It has to be terribly hidden away, else Mark or somebody is bound to see her in time."

"It's all right. This place has a high brick wall around and fierce dogs to keep people out."

"Wherever is it?"

"It's Mr. Dermot's."

"Mr. Dermot's!" Christina stopped in her tracks a second time. "You mean—the—the secret? You said he was dead."

"Oh, well, I just said that because you were prying. He isn't dead."

"That's where you go, isn't it? When you go out all day. I knew there was somewhere special. The flying-machine man."

"How do you know he's a flying-machine man?"

"Oh, don't you remember? When a man delivered the book, and Uncle threw it in the fire. It was from Mr. Dermot."

"Yes, of course. Oh, well, you know all about him."

"No, that's absolutely all I know. His name, and that he encourages you in flying."

"I don't mind your knowing so much now. Because if you mention it to Mark or Father, I shall tell them why I took you there."

"Blackmail," said Christina. But it was perfectly fair. She was very pleased that she was going to be let into William's secret, and immensely curious.

"Who is he, then?"

"Just a man."

"With a family?"

"No. A bachelor."

"Old? Young?"

"Oh, middling, I suppose."

"And he flies?"

"*He* doesn't fly. He has built an aircraft. Someone else flies it."

"You?" said Christina, for a joke.

William grinned. "He can't fly," he explained, "because he has very bad eyesight. If he were to get up to twenty-five feet he wouldn't be able to see the ground any more. Anyway, you will meet him. I will introduce you. And you can eat all your words about flying, when you see what he has done."

"Oh, that was three years ago, when I first met you. I know it works now, because of what I've seen in the newspapers. Mr. Blériot's flying the Channel last year quite convinced me."

"Good."

"How did you meet Mr. Dermot? No one else has ever heard of him."

"Oh yes, they have. Not your fox-chasing maniacs, though; perhaps they aren't interested in anything else but foxes, but civilized people know his work all right. I met him when I was ten, when I fell off a horse once. The horse galloped on and I called at the nearest house, which was Mr. Dermot's. He had a car in the drive, and I was interested and he took me for a drive. It was wonderful. He was the first proper person I had ever met. Intelligent, I mean, with a proper sense of values. And interested in me, too, that was the best thing of all. As if I were a human being, instead of just the worst rider the Russells had ever bred. He told me to come again, and he would show me his glider. Oh, it was marvelous, I can tell you!"

William's face was animated with enthusiasm, his eyes shining.

"And you've been there lots since?" Christina said.

"Oh, yes, several times a week the last year or two. I walk there and drive back in the car with Joe. Joe is Mr. Dermot's mechanic."

"But hasn't anyone ever seen you? Why hasn't Uncle ever found out, or Mark?"

"I'm jolly careful, Christina. It's no joke with me, this, you know." William turned very solemn. "I take great care. In the car, for example, I get dropped off at Creephedge Lane— you know it? It's almost a mile from Flambards. And when I'm driving I muffle myself up with a cap and goggles and scarf so that if I passed Mark he wouldn't know it was me."

"And if Uncle were to find out—?"

"He's bound to stop me going. Probably give me the whole of Baily's Directory to learn by heart, and an almighty swishing to help me on with it. But I've worked it out. I'm sixteen now. If I can keep it up for another year or two, it won't matter if he does find out. If he throws me out I shall be a good enough mechanic to get a job. And what I've learned through knowing Mr. Dermot he can never undo, whatever he does to me."

The conversation was interrupted at this point when Dick

came into sight, riding Cherry and leading Sweetbriar. He dismounted, and changed Sweetbriar's bridle for an old rope halter.

"I'll have to take the bridle back, miss. But you'll be all right with this. Mr. Mark has taken Treasure down to the blacksmith—that'll take him the rest of the morning, so you shouldn't be seen."

"Are you sure it's all right, Dick?" Having come to the point, Christina felt anything but confident that her plan would go undiscovered.

"I'll carry on to Lucas' and have a word with the kennelman. I know him well enough. We can probably fix it, in case any questions are asked."

"Do you want any money?" William asked astutely.

"I shall give him the price of a drink," Dick said.

William passed over some coins, which Dick, after a fraction's hesitation, accepted.

"Thank you very much, sir." He paused and added, "She's going somewhere—kindly, like? At her age, and in her condition, being shot isn't necessarily a bad thing."

William looked at Christina. Christina hesitated. She had Sweetbriar's halter in her hand, and as she hesitated the mare turned her head and pushed her pink nose softly into Christina's hand. Her eyes were mild and contented. She stood quietly, asking nothing.

Christina said firmly, "She'll have a very good home."

"They're much kinder where she's going than they are at Flambards," William said, smiling.

Dick mounted Cherry again, and gathered up his reins. He was smiling too. "The horses are all right at Flambards," he said. He did not put into words the obvious conclusion to this statement, but all three of them were aware of it.

"It's just the human beings . . ." William finished for him, after he had ridden away.

"This is it," William said.

Christina was relieved, more used to riding than walking,

when William pointed out a gateway ahead. Although they were in a back lane which led nowhere, well off the main road, the gates were impressive, set in a high new brick wall. William opened them, and Christina led Sweetbriar through. Inside, the gravel drive curved away between thick woods on either hand, which Christina was sure must be full of good foxes. Curious, and slightly nervous, she led the mare along behind William, until a final wriggle of the drive revealed the front of a small stone Georgian house with a white-painted front door. To the left of the house was a cobbled stableyard, where two cars stood, one on either side of the trough; to the right of the house a big new barn had been built, with doors that opened out into a large field where a herd of heifers grazed. Behind the house there seemed to be more outbuildings and an old orchard. There was no garden, but the grass all around was neatly mown and some early crocuses were showing through. The whole picture was neat and uneccentric, not at all what Christina had been expecting.

Two men were working on one of the cars. They waved cheerfully to William and one of them shouted. "The old man's indoors." But at that moment the front door opened and someone who Christina assumed was the old man himself came out. Not that he gave the impression of great age; he was spry, almost gnomish-looking, with tufty iron-gray hair and gold-rimmed spectacles through which he peered eagerly, as if anxious not to miss anything. His clothes were certainly unusual. He wore a large navy-blue jersey like a sailor's, black pin-striped trousers, and a leather jacket without sleeves.

"Ah, Will," he said, sounding pleased. "We've solved that trouble with the carburetor. Lunch is almost ready. What's that?" He lifted his head like a pointer and peered down through his spectacles. "A horse?"

"Yes. And this is my cousin, Christina," William said.

"How do you do," Christina said politely.

"Very pleased to meet you, my dear. You may stay to lunch." He looked at Sweetbriar again. "I don't know about the horse, though."

"It was going to be shot," William explained. "And we brought it here to save its life. I hoped you wouldn't mind."

"No, indeed. I wouldn't like to see it shot. Joe will see to it. It can eat the orchard. Joe!"

One of the men from under the car scrambled out and came up. "You understand horses, don't you? Could you manage this one? It's to live here, I take it?" he asked William.

"If you don't mind," William said.

"Oh, yes, she's nice," Joe said appreciatively. "She can go in the box next to the motorcar. There's plenty of hay and straw that we got for the heifers. And she can go in the orchard daytime, keep that grass down."

"There," said Mr. Dermot. "I knew Joe would understand."

"Her name is Sweetbriar," Christina said, handing over the halter.

"There. Now, you'll stay to lunch? Come along in."

Mr. Dermot led the way into the house. Christina, fascinated by this sudden new world, was enchanted by everything she saw: the gleaming white interior of the austere house; pale, shining wood floors with rugs like jewels, and fine modern furniture. Everything was spacious, of a fastidious male taste, nothing unnecessary; there was no bric-a-brac or ornamentation. There were books, in book shelves from ceiling to floor, and sumptuous curtains of fantastic oriental colors. By the window in the big living room a table was laid, very simply. Christina had never seen such plain cutlery away from the kitchen, yet from the marks she could see that it was real silver.

Mr. Dermot took her coat and hat, and Christina said, "Oh, it's lovely!" She could not help passing the remark. Perhaps after Flambards, she thought, anything would seem lovely, and yet this house was like no other she had ever seen.

Mr. Dermot rubbed his hands and smiled. "You like it? Good. This room, I find, is very good for thinking in. Restful. Not distracting in any way. Afterward you will see the study, where we work. That is very different, I'm afraid. Eh, William?"

"Oh, I like it best of all," William said.

"From this window," Mr. Dermot said, "we have a view

of our airfield—yes, I mean where the heifers are grazing. We keep them just to keep the grass down for our little kite. And when we sit here, Christina, we have visions of our little kite skimming over those trees at the bottom and up into that marvelous sky. Soon . . . by the summer, eh, William? At the moment, our record is a hundred yards, at a height of six feet."

"Oh, but most of them at Brooklands are doing no better yet," William said. "After all, it's only six months since the first circular mile—British, that is," he added for Christina's benefit. "We're badly behind the Americans, and the French. But *Emma* will do the most beautiful circles, if only we can get her off the ground."

"*Emma?*"

"Our machine. We have great faith in our design," Mr. Dermot said, "if only we can get it to fly."

Christina would have laughed at this paradox, but sensed in time that it was not meant to be funny.

"It's engine power we're short on," William explained, and he then digressed into engine talk which did not include Christina, and left her time to digest her impressions, and watch Mr. Dermot's manservant serve the meal. He was so much more accomplished than Mary, who banged everything down in a great hurry; Christina watched him happily, sitting in a little cocoon of sensuous delight at such luxury, her mind stretched and amazed at everything she saw, and everything she heard. And as the meal progressed she became aware of William as an absolutely different person from the William she knew—a William as talkative as Mark after a day's hunting. He was no longer a boy. He had an authority Christina had never sensed before. He leaned over the table talking— and it could have been a foreign language for all Christina understood of it—and his face was alive, his manner with Mr. Dermot full of confidence and trust. For the first time Christina noticed that his fingers were stained with oil all around the fingernails (Mr. Dermot's hands were graven with black lines, the skin stretched gray, although they were freshly washed). Mr. Dermot treated William as an equal, with courtesy and respect. William's own father had never so much as spared him one glance of affection, Christina realized painfully, while Mr. Dermot listened, and nodded, and smiled. Christina remembered William muttering "Mr. Dermot" in his sleep, the night she had found him walking on his broken leg, and the whole mystery of William's friendship was now laid out before her very eyes.

"Are you going to fly Emma?" she asked William.

William glanced at Mr. Dermot and said, "Yes."

Mr. Dermot smiled.

"But it's very dangerous," Christina pointed out. "You might easily get killed. Who was it, a few weeks ago?"

"Delagrange."

"Yes. Well, suppose you got killed flying?"

"You can suppose anything," William said, very rationally.

"Suppose you get killed hunting? My father encourages you to hunt. If Mr. Dermot permits me to fly, I see no difference. In any case, if it's my father you're thinking about, why should he care if I get killed? He was happy enough to try to kill me hunting."

"William won't get killed, I think, if we don't get any higher off the ground than six feet," Mr. Dermot said dryly. "Not yet awhile."

"But she *will* fly, soon," William said. "And then I will fly her." He looked anxiously at Mr. Dermot.

Mr. Dermot gave a little shrug. "Perhaps." He turned to Christina gravely, and said, "William's father now . . . is he such a terrible man as William makes out to me? It puzzles me."

"I don't know what William has told you, but I should think it is the truth," Christina said. "Mr. Russell doesn't seem to care what William does." It sounded brutal. She tried to condone him. "He is a sick man since his accident."

"He cares about Mark, though. And you too," William said.

Christina suddenly saw, by William's expression, what it meant to him to be unwanted in his own home. For a fleeting moment, his face was quite bare with pain. She realized that, unlike herself, William had not been an outcast all his life, only—presumably—since his mother had died when he was nine, and his father had had his accident the following year. He had been a witness to his father's accident; Christina could well believe that his own father had in fact put William off hunting, for getting himself mangled before the boy's very eyes. The irony of it shook her, watching William. She felt a great pity for him, having had to learn not to belong, instead of—like her—just growing up not belonging.

But whatever William lacked at home, Christina came to realize that he had found a true friend in Mr. Dermot. She was shown the study, where they "worked together," as Mr. Dermot explained, and she noticed all the books on mathematics laid open on the desk, and the copybooks full of William's quick, spiderish calculations. Books were everywhere; the walls

were covered with working drawings of aircraft wings, the floor
and windowsills littered with bits of engine. Then they went
outside to the big barn, and Mr. Dermot pulled back the door
to reveal *Emma*, the beloved flying machine.

"We won't wheel her out. It's too windy today," he said.

She was quite small and frail, and Christina understood his
concern. There were two wings of closely woven fabric
stretched over wooden frames which showed through like the
veins of dragonfly wings, and a fuselage of wooden hoops
joined with long struts of spruce. The pilot's seat was a
wooden board nailed across the fuselage struts, and in front of
it the engine was mounted, a strange tangled contraption of
cylinders and wires sitting incongruously between the out-
stretched wing spans. The aircraft stood on three bicycle
wheels, and even in the shed the drafts made faint whistling
noises in her struts, and her wings swayed slightly, as if she
would like to go.

Christina admired her, finding words with difficulty, for she
did not know what to think about the outlandish machine. To
her eyes, if she were truthful, it looked ridiculous, and highly
dangerous.

"I would love to see it fly."

"Oh, yes, so would we," William replied. "If you like, you
could come over on a still day, and we will show you what she
can do."

Mr. Dermot smiled happily. "A month or two—and I think
we will get her over the trees, Will."

They went around to the stables, where Sweetbriar was now
comfortably installed in a stall beside the Rolls-Royce.

"I'll look after her, miss, never you fear," Joe told her. He
was a little older than Dick, with an intelligent gleam in his
eyes. Both he and his brother wore oil-black caps and overalls
shining with grease. Watching them, Christina had a strange
premonition that these quick, clever brothers, wiping their
hands on lumps of black rags, were the grooms of a coming
generation: for the first time it struck her that perhaps
William was not as mad as she had always believed, to be

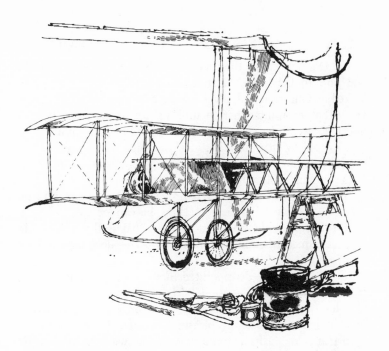

putting his faith in motorcars and flying machines: that they might, indeed, work. Her eyes widened at the prospect. The future William saw danced before her eyes, with everyone traveling by motor, or soaring over the countryside on their dragonfly wings. Not only William, but Mr. Dermot, and Joe and Jack, believed in this future. She could see their devotion in their eyes, just as in Dick and Fowler she saw the ingrained, inborn faith in the horse. And who was right? Before today she had never known these possibilities existed, but these people were not fools; she felt humbled by their faith, excited by their courage; her mind all shaken up, inspired, suddenly confused. Just for a moment the visions dazzled her. It was like the moment with Dick, when, for a fleeting period of time, everything was seen with an extra dimension. After it, she felt she had grown older and wiser and yet, in all essence, nothing had changed. William had got down and disappeared under the Rolls-Royce, looking at something with Joe, and she was still standing by Sweetbriar, the reason for her being there.

Mr. Dermot patted the mare absently, glanced at his watch, and said to Christina, "I must go and do some work." He looked at Christina and, although he did not say anything, she knew that he wanted her to walk up to the house with him. She left Sweetbriar's side and fell into step beside him.

"I'm glad William brought you," he said. "He always said he would. But not Mark. They are very different, as brothers?"

"Yes. Quite different."

"Is it true that the father hates William? William says he does, but perhaps there is something he cannot see."

"I think he is disappointed in him, that is the reason. He isn't very nice to him. I think perhaps he does almost hate him."

"For a man to be disappointed in a son of William's caliber is beyond my comprehension," Mr. Dermot said, with a sad twitch of a smile. "He has the most brilliant mathematical brain it has ever been my pleasure to teach. He could have a scholarship to Oxford tomorrow, if he wished. Which he doesn't, I might add. I told him I would speak to his father, but he is absolutely determined to keep us apart."

Christina agreed with William on this. The two men scarcely spoke the same language. Russell would merely become abusive.

"You cannot imagine how different he is from William," she tried to explain. "He is a—a violent man. He is not inter- ested in anything apart from hunting, and if he could not understand you, he would shout at you. It is quite different at Flambards, from here."

They stood before the white front door, and she looked into the shining, civilized house—and it seemed to her at that moment that it truly did shine, with kindliness and reason and light. By contrast Flambards suddenly seemed all darkness, violence, and ignorance. She remembered Dick, and his parting remark, and knew that it was true.

"The horses get the best of everything at Flambards," she said gravely.

Mr. Dermot laughed. "Perhaps Will should grow a mane and tail, then." Then he grew serious again, and said, "He will make his own way. Perhaps it is best to leave things as they are. He is as welcome here, always, as any son of mine could be. And you, too, my dear, if you wish:" He smiled again. "William says that although you are a hunting Russell, there is still hope for you. I think he means it as a great compliment."

Christina smiled.

There was a honking noise behind them and the loud putter of a single-cylinder engine, and the bright green de Dion with William at the wheel came at a dashing pace along the gravel from the stables, and scrunched to a smart halt beside Christina. Joe sat in the back seat, and William made an elaborate gesture toward the empty seat beside him and said, "Madam, your carriage awaits you."

"Good gracious! Are you going to drive?"

"Certainly, madam."

"You can trust him," Mr. Dermot said, grinning. "He's a very reliable chauffeur. One of the best I've ever had."

Christina got up dubiously. William smiled and said, "It's not a flying machine, girl! Anyone would think from your face that you don't trust us."

"I don't," said Christina.

"I'm afraid she's hopelessly old-fashioned," William apologized to Mr. Dermot. "She thinks because there is no horse that it can't possibly go. Christina, it's nineteen hundred and ten. Motorcars have existed for fifteen years now. And they do work."

"You show her," said Mr. Dermot.

"Certainly, I will. She needs educating. Look, Christina, you could drive this motor. It's so easy."

He moved a lever which stuck up beside the steering wheel, let off the brake, and they were suddenly moving away down the drive. Mr. Dermot waved, laughing. Christina, holding on to a little brass rail at her side, saw nothing before her but a shining engine cover and the spattering gravel. It was very noisy, and smelly, but the trees were bowling past. They were at the gates in no time. William came to a smooth halt, and

Joe got down to open them. Already Christina was impressed. William drove through, and waited for Joe to shut them and climb up again.

"He's the postilion," he said with a grin.

Once more he moved the lever and stamped on a pedal on the floor, and the car moved off down the lane, bouncing and full of energy. They came down under the still naked trees, shaking in the ruts, to a turning onto a paved road, and there William moved his levers once more, stamped on his pedals, and drove the de Dion with a look on his face that reminded Christina of Mark putting Treasure at a big fence when hounds had a view. She braced her knees, full of apprehension, gasping at the cold wind that whirled her hair around her shoulders and watered her eyes. The elms spun past; the bare plow was a speeding corrugation with, somewhere, a man's face gaping and a cart horse tossing its head with a wild eye.

"Twenty-seven, Joe!" William called back over his shoulder.

"Twenty-seven what?" Christina gasped.

"Miles per hour."

"No faster than a horse!" Christina shouted stubbornly.

William laughed. He had his cap on backward, and the wild wind had put color in his cheeks. Christina wondered what would happen if they met Mark, and laughed. She caught William's exhilaration, and watched the road dive down into the valley like a gray ribbon before them, and was not afraid when William did not brake. The little motor rattled and bounced and William glanced at her, grinning.

"Steady on, Will!" said Joe from the back.

"You're scared!"

"For Mr. Dermot's motor!" Joe shouted back.

But William changed gear, and the motorcar went more sedately, bowling down the hill. Christina noticed how awkwardly William had to sit to accommodate his stiff leg, and wondered how he could manage at all. He had obviously had plenty of practice. The five miles dropped away, and William parked discreetly off the road still some way from Flambards, and turned off the engine regretfully.

"There, Joe, she's all yours,"

Joe swung himself over into the driving seat.

"Right thruster, isn't he, miss?" he said cheerfully. "If that flying machine ever gets off the ground, I reckon you'll be a holy terror, Will."

"I can't wait," William said.

Joe turned the de Dion around and disappeared back the way they had come, and William and Christina started walking the last mile to the gates of Flambards.

"Do you always drive back?" Christina asked.

"Nearly always."

"And are you really going to fly this aircraft, when it's ready?"

"All the flying she's done so far, I was in her. Sometimes Joe has a go, and sometimes Mr. Dermot, but I've done the best in her."

"Mr. Dermot said, 'Perhaps.' Not that you can. Only 'perhaps.'"

"Oh, he knows I will," William said.

Christina was silent. She felt she had learned a great deal about William today. It seemed more like a week than a few hours since they had met Dick with Sweetbriar. They walked on, not saying anything, and soon the gates of Flambards were in sight.

Just Like Old Times

The hunting season finished. Christina went to the point-to-point races and saw Mark finish second on Treasure, and had to console him for the mistake that cost him the winner's cup.

"The fool horse just didn't lift himself for that last hedge. Went right through it and nearly came down. . . ."

Christina, who had been watching, knew that Treasure, tiring fast, would have jumped if he had been pulled together and given a word of encouragement, instead of the wild spurring he had actually received, but she did not say this to Mark. "You did splendidly! I don't know what you're so cross about. You're bound to win next year, or the year after."

"Oh, next year . . ." Mark growled. He looked just like his father when he was angry, the dark eyes almost disappearing under black eyebrows.

The following weekend he went to the Hunt Ball, and came home very drunk in the early hours of the morning. He had offered to take Christina, but Christina had refused, partly because she had no dress to wear and partly because Mary had said she was too young. When she saw Mark the following morning, she was glad she had stayed away.

Two days later Mark went over to Thornton's and came home with the chestnut he had coveted, Goldwillow, a beautifully made whole-colored horse, with a mane and tail the same dark red as his coat. Fowler and the boys were full of admiration and excitement, and Mark came in for lunch glowing with well-being. Over lunch the conversation was exclusively about Goldwillow. William, when he had finished, pushed back his chair and left the table, but Christina stayed to pour the coffee. They seemed to spend a lot of time talking about horses when hunting was finished; there seemed to be a lot of time to fill. Outside it was raining, with a wild spring wind buffeting the loose window sashes.

Mark put a splash of brandy in his coffee, and tilted back his chair, holding it with his knee against the table. Suddenly, remembering something, he came down with a crash that spilled his coffee.

"I say. I've just remembered! I found out a deuced queer thing this morning."

"What's that?" Russell asked.

"Well, when I was at Thornton's, Lucas was there. And just to be polite, I said something about the mare we sent over, and he didn't seem to know anything about it. Said there was nothing from Flambards that he knew of. I couldn't make it out."

"Lucas spends plenty of time in the kennels. If he didn't see her I reckon she didn't go," Russell said shortly. "You'd better have a word with Fowler. Who was supposed to take her?"

"Dick."

"Have a word with Dick, then. These lads aren't above a deal on the side, if they think they can get away with it. We can see to it now, if you like. Go and get Dick."

"Oh, Father, let me get my coffee," Mark grumbled.

Christina pushed back her chair.

"I'll go," she said, trying to keep her voice level. "I've finished."

They scarcely looked up. Mark said, "Good," and tipped his chair back again, and Christina slipped out. She closed the door behind her, and leaned on it for a moment to get her breath which seemed to have got stuck in her throat. She was shivering all over and cold as ice. Never, not since the first day in her life that she could remember, had she felt so afraid. She heard Mark laugh, and saw him pushing his chair back, strong and arrogant. He had the power of God over Dick.

She put on her coat, and went out into the rain. The chestnuts were holding out great skirts of candled flowers that rocked against the clouds, full of promise. Christina turned away from them and ran, feeling the cold wind lifting the heaviness of her hair. In the stables it was quiet and warm. Dick was in the box with the new horse, Goldwillow, tipping a feed into the scrubbed manger. The other boys were eating their bread-and-dripping in the tack room.

"Oh, Dick!" Christina did not know how to tell him.

"What's wrong, miss?" Dick turned from the horse in surprise. He gave her a long, slow look, and his expression changed, very slowly. He held the empty sieve in one hand and stroked Goldwillow with the other, pursing his lips slightly.

"What is it?"

"They know. They want to see you."

Dick did not say anything. He put a hand under the chestnut's roller to smooth a wrinkle, gave him another pat, and came out of the door.

"I'll fetch my jacket."

Christina waited, still shivering. Dick came out of the tack room buttoning his jacket, and they walked up the drive together.

"How did they find out?"

Christina told him.

"Did you say anything?"

"No."

Christina's fear increased with every step, but Dick's face showed nothing.

"Does it mean you—you will lose your job?" she managed to squeeze out.

"Yes," Dick said.

"Dick, I—" Christina could not find any words that meant anything. They reached the door, and Dick waited for Christina to go in ahead of him, and took off his cap, showing the gold hair that never ceased to surprise Christina, even now.

"But it was my fault, Dick. Not yours."

"Oh, no. It was mine. I knew what I was doing," Dick said.

They crossed the hall and Dick knocked at the dining-room door. Mark shouted, "Come in." Dick went in, shutting the door behind him.

Christina knew that she should walk in right behind Dick and tell Russell that the whole business was her fault, but she couldn't. And yet she knew that she must. She stood outside the door, her breath choking her. She put her hand on the door handle. From inside she heard Mark say, "Oh, don't tell lies!" A tremor of pure agony went through Christina.

"What on earth's the matter?"

Christina spun round. In all this extremity of feeling, she had quite forgotten the existence of William, who now stood at the bottom of the stairs in his walking clothes, ready to go out.

"Mark's found out about Sweetbriar. They've got Dick in there now! And I must tell them it was my fault, else he'll get the sack. And I'm too scared! I can't!" She started to cry, white-faced and shaking.

"Oh, heavens! What a mess!" William said heavily. He looking at Christina thoughtfully, then he said, "Oh, it's not that bad, Christina. Not for us. Only for Dick. Look, we'll try, but I'm afraid Dick's for the drop." He hesitated, while Christina groped for a handkerchief and wiped her face. "All right?"

She nodded.

"Advance," said William.

He reached over and opened the door and went in with her. Christina found, to her infinite relief, that she had a small reserve of courage left in her, for she was able to face Russell squarely across the table, and all her trembling stopped. Russell was clearly in a towering rage. Anything that happened behind his back and which he only found out through accident infuriated him out of all proportion to its gravity, for it reminded him of his uselessness. What Dick had said Christina did not know, for she said immediately, "It was my fault. I asked Dick to do it."

"And since when have you been giving orders around here?" Russell said acidly.

"Only that once. I didn't want Sweetbriar to be killed."

"What you want is of no account here. In any case, it makes no difference. Dick knows who gives the orders around here. Don't you?"

"Yes, sir."

"You can leave at once. Ask Fowler for your money. And don't expect me to write any letters for you. I've no word for dishonest servants."

"Dick's not dishonest!" Christina cried out. "There's nobody in Flambards more honest than Dick! How can you say such a thing? I asked him to do it. He did it for me. I know I was wrong, but it's not fair to treat him so harshly." Christina's fear was completely blotted out now by the rage for the injustice that was being done. She felt William take her elbow, urgently, pulling her back from the table, and saw Russell's face start to deepen in color. Mark was leaning forward, his eyes full of malicious enjoyment.

"And why is Dick so eager to do your favor?" Mark asked. "How do you pay him for that? I thought—"

Dick stepped forward, his cheeks flushing as dangerously as Russell's, but William cut in, hissing at Mark, "Don't judge others by yourself!" He turned abruptly and said softly to Dick, "Don't say anything! Get out! Don't stay and be mauled!"

"And what have you got to do with all this?" Mark shot at William, getting to his feet. "Whom are you protecting?"

"I'm protecting no one," William said contemptuously. "Only trying to get you to behave like a human being. Christina is right. Dick does not deserve to be treated like this. He was wrong, but we were worse. We asked him to do it, and I took Sweetbriar away. You've no right not to give him references."

"Are you talking to me?" Russell's voice rolled in his throat like a clap of thunder. Christina felt her loyal, indignant heart sink with an awful premonition of disaster.

"Yes, I am," William said, as if realizing, like Christina, that there was no going back.

"You took Sweetbriar away?"

"Yes."

"You knew what my orders were?"

"Yes. So if you want to punish someone, punish me. But leave Dick alone!"

"My God, so I will!" Russell said. He sat in his chair, breathing heavily, fumbling for his crutches. "You insolent whelp! You useless milksop! It's time you had some guts thrashed into you."

Red flecks danced in Russell's cheeks. His eyes were bloodshot, and he swore terribly as he tried to get up from his chair. Christina watched in horror. She utterly despised him at that moment; his brutality was primitive, a reckless vengeance for what life had done to him, meaningless as a child's rage.

To her own amazement, she found a voice.

"Haven't you done enough to William?" she cried out. "And Dick, too? I started all this, about Sweetbriar! What are you going to do to me?"

She saw Mark's face explode with delight, then Russell hit her with his crutch—a blow across the shoulder that sent her sprawling. His voice roared in her ears. His stick crashed on the floor, then flew up in Mark's direction. Mark ducked.

"Fetch me a cane!" Russell roared. "I'll beat the lot of you! I'll show you who gives orders around here. Get your trousers down, Will! Get over that chair, you one-legged chicken!"

His crutch crashed on the mahogany table. Christina, sick with the blow she had caught, buried her head in the cushions of an armchair and started to sob. She put her hands over her head to shut out the dreadful swish and bite of the cane and put her teeth in the cushion to stop them chattering. But all the time she could hear Russell grunting and swearing and

muttering his maniac's invective between the blows. He
sounded like a madman. She put her fingers in her ears, and
her hands were wet with fright.

At last, he flung the cane on the floor and banged on the
table with his crutch.

"Get me a drink, Mark! Or do you want a dose too? It
wouldn't hurt you! And you!" The voice swung in Christina's
direction. "Stop your sniveling and get up! I've done with
thrashing for today. Get up, d'you hear me! I'm giving the
orders for a change."

Christina lifted her head cautiously. The room swam. She

took a steady breath and got to her feet. It was as if the waves of violence that had shattered the peace of the weekday afternoon were running out, dying, making their final tremors in the shaking of her own hands. She put her palms together, and looked at Russell. The dreadful purple had died out of his face. He was taking his drink from Mark, his rage spent in the physical satisfaction of beating William. Dick had gone. William was fastening his suspenders, his face shining with sweat. Mark said to him, "D'you want a drink?" and William nodded.

"Then get out, all of you," Russell said. "You make me tired."

He sat down heavily in his chair, and gestured to Mark to put the brandy bottle down beside him. He looked gray and ill. Christina walked cautiously around him to join the two boys, and they left the room together in silence. Mark shut the door quietly and the three of them stood in the hall, looking at one another.

"Much good it did me, being noble," William said bitterly. "I shan't be able to sit down for a week."

"Fortnight, I should say," Mark said affably. "Just like old times, wasn't it?"

Christina could think of nothing to say at all. She felt spent, as if it were she who had had the beating, and her head ached. Her mind felt sour with disgust.

"If I'd known what the outcome was going to be, I wouldn't have said anything," Mark said.

"Dick," Christina said, tightly.

"Oh, I'm not bothered about Dick. But that was a tough beating. And I bet Will—and Dick, too—only did it because you badgered him." Mark looked at Christina, not in any way accusing, but slightly amused. His words, brutally true, cut into Christina. Her face quivered. She knew that it was the truth, and she was appalled. She looked bleakly at William, and William, seeing her distress, gave her a difficult smile and said, "Look, Christina, I did ask for it, didn't I?"

"I'll say," said Mark, pleased. "And I reckon Christina did

too, come to that. If you'd been male, you'd have got it too. It shows Father still has a shred of decency left—that he only threw the crutch at you, I mean."

Mark grinned. For him, the incident was over. He whistled to one of the foxhounds and went out of the front door. William turned to go back up the stairs.

"Were you going to Mr. Dermot's?" Christina asked.

"Yes. But I don't feel much like it now."

Christina went upstairs with him, trying not to cry again. "Will, I'm sorry. Not that it's any use—but I'm sorry."

"Don't worry about it," William said. "Look, truly, it doesn't matter any more. Once it would have. But now it's different. He can hurt me physically, but he can't hurt me any other way, now. And even that—you'd be surprised, if you put your mind to it. I just shut my eyes, and every time a wallop comes I say to myself, 'Mr. Dermot,' and next time. 'Emma,' and next time, 'flying.' And 'Emma' and 'flying' and 'Mr. Dermot' and it just doesn't seem to matter at all. Truly, Christina—not just boasting. So don't feel bad for me." He stopped at the top of the stairs and the conviction went out of his eyes. "Only for Dick, Christina. He's got no Mr. Dermot."

Christina went down to the stables, when she had summoned up enough courage. She felt cold and sick, and wished she were dead. The rain had stopped and the sun had come out. The stableyard was freshly washed and gleaming and a boy was whistling somewhere. Fowler was in the feed shed, standing by the thresher.

"Mr. Fowler," Christina said. Her voice was barely above a whisper. "Where's Dick?"

"He's gone, miss," Fowler said. Christina realized that Fowler wasn't doing anything, but just standing in the gloom of the feed shed, out of the way. She saw that he had a tear on his cheek. The sight of it was like another blow from Russell's crutch, to send flying the remnants of any crumb of comfort. She stood against the wall, unable to say anything else.

"He did not deserve it," Fowler said, "not with what he has

to bear already, at home. And he was a good boy, the best I've ever had here. It's a wicked shame, to dismiss a boy like Dick."

"Would—would you—could you tell Mr. Russell that?" Christina whispered.

Fowler reflected, and shook his head. "No, miss. I'm too old to face Mr. Russell again. I know Mr. Russell. I've my own place to consider." He shook his head briskly, and turned to the feed bins, as if that was what he was about.

"If Dick is so good, he will get another job, with a better employer than Mr. Russell," Christina said steadily.

Fowler turned back to her again. "What makes you think that?" he asked. "He's been sent away with a reputation for cheating Mr. Lucas out of five pounds' worth of good horse-flesh. None of the hunting folk will want him, Mr. Lucas will see to that. Jobs of any kind are scarce just now, and a job with good horses like we have here is one in a thousand. Dick is in rare trouble, take it from me, Miss Christina. He acted very silly, I don't deny, but he's going to pay for it."

"It was my fault," Christina whispered.

"Yes, I've eyes in my head," Fowler said shortly. "I can see how it happened."

Christina went blindly back to the house. She went up to William's room, and found him lying on his bed, face down. He opened his eyes to see who it was, but said nothing. Christina went to the window and leaned against the wooden frame, looking down across the tangled garden and to the woods beyond. The oaks were frosted with pale new leaf, bright against the dark fir. The sun shone warmly, full of promise. Christina pressed her damp, burning face against the glass, and ached for what she had done.

The Quiet One

In the weeks that followed, Christina could not bring herself to ask Violet about Dick. She knew from the stables that he was out of work, but no more.

She asked Mary. "What is this trouble at home, that Fowler mentioned?"

"It's been hard for them both," Mary said. "Their father died some years ago and they have a mother who is sick. She's not old; she's only just in her forties, but she has a paralysis in her legs. She was knocked over by a cart, and her spine was damaged. She's a nice woman, never complains, but she's in a great deal of pain, and she should have medicine and good food. Well, you can imagine, on what Dick and Violet earn, it's always been a struggle. I dare say it was a struggle even when their father was alive, for he drank most of what he earned. And between you and me, Violet's a flighty piece. I reckon it's Dick who keeps that family going. What will happen to them now, I don't know."

"Does my uncle know all this?"

"Yes, I should think so. It's always been the same, the last ten years or so. The father used to work for Mr. Russell, too, before Dick."

"Does Mark know?"

"He must. The family has always lived in the village. Everyone knows them."

Christina tackled Mark, but knew she was doomed, from the start.

"What do you expect me to do?" he asked, in honest exasperation. "Dick should have thought of all this before he was so stupid. Anyone would have sacked him for what he did. You don't expect me to take him back, do you?"

"Can't you find him another job? Or give him some decent references?"

"But everyone knows what has happened now. I'm not stopping anyone else employing him, am I? It just hasn't anything to do with me any more."

"If Mr. Lucas put in a word for him—"

"But why should he? Dick did him out of a good deal of money. Hounds don't feed on air, do they? Lucas has to buy flesh, and when he gets a horse free, it's a good day for him."

"But Dick's mother—"

"Oh, for heaven's sake, Christina! There's always the poorhouse for people like that. What's it got to do with me? Dick should have thought. I wouldn't have him back now for a hundred pounds. In fact, he always did make me cross with his sly ways. I'm glad he's gone. And anyway," he added, after a slight pause, "why are you so concerned about him?"

"Because it was all my fault. I feel responsible. You wouldn't understand," she added cuttingly.

"No. There are some reasons I would understand. But not that one. Not for a servant." He spoke to annoy, stressing the first sentence suggestively.

Christina flounced away, furious. "You have no—no feelings at all! You are like an animal!"

"I like animals," Mark said, grinning.

Another fortnight passed and Christina knew that Dick still had no job. William explained; "Even farming, the farmers won't take him because they want to keep in with Mr. Lucas. It's always like that. When Father was active, if someone offended him and was sent away, the poor devil would have to go to another part of the country to get a job, because no one dared take him on, for fear of Father. And besides,

Christina, there aren't many spare jobs going for the working
classes. Dick is not the only man out of work in the village."

"Perhaps, if I go to see him, I could help."

"I wouldn't," William said.

But Christina was obsessed by Dick's plight. It would have
been bad enough if it had been none of her doing, but the
fact that Dick's suffering was due entirely to her own thought-
lessness lay on her conscience like a dark cloud. She could
enjoy nothing. It was useless to try to explain to Mark how
she felt about Dick. It was certainly love that she felt for him,
in one of its innumerable shades of meaning, but not the
love that Mark hinted at. Over the three years she had received more kindness and consideration from Dick than from
anybody else in Flambards, and she had shared most of her
fears and happinesses with him too. He was gentle and kind,
qualities that Christina had come to rate highly. And she
missed him, more than she had thought possible. In spite of
William's advice, she went down to the village one afternoon
to call.

She did not know where he lived, and had to ask. She felt
embarrassed, inquiring at the post office, and distinctly hesitant
when the house was pointed out to her. It was one in a row
of clapboard cottages, extremely shabby, with the paint bare
and several slates missing from the roof. There was a short
front garden full of rank grass and a path made of ashes. Christina approached nervously. The curtains were in rags and faded
white. Her heart sank.

The door was partly open. She knocked.

"Come in."

Dick was standing in front of the range, stirring a saucepan
that bubbled over the flames. He had one elbow up on the
mantelshelf, and was leaning his head on his forearm, cooking
as if he cared little for what he was doing. His breeches were
covered in dried mud, his shirt was dirty; he was unshaven,
and needed a haircut. He looked around absently from the
fire, and started to say something. Then he saw who it was.

He jumped around with an expression of horror flooding over his face. The color flared in his cheeks.

"Miss Christina!"

His shocked face put Christina at a disadvantage. Already nervous, she was dismayed by the evidence of Dick's poverty. She had always thought the little village cottages picturesque, but there was nothing picturesque about the interior of this one, with its sagging, damp-stained ceiling and floor of broken flagstones. There were a rickety table and two hard chairs, no other furniture. There was no sink or tap, only a pail of water standing under the window, and a bowl on the floor with some dirty dishes in it. The walls were mildewed and dark with damp almost up to the ceiling, the whitewash clinging in wet flakes. Christina could not help her eyes going around, nor the dismay showing in her face; yet she knew enough to realize that she was hurting him, by intruding on his poverty.

"What do you want?" he asked. His voice was hard. He looked very tired, with deep shadows under his eyes.

Christina was at a complete loss. "I—I—" She wondered, suddenly, what did she want? Too late, she knew it had been a mistake to come.

"I wanted to help," she said softly.

Dick shrugged. "This is no place for you. We are managing. There is nothing you can do."

"Because it was my fault."

"I told you before, I knew what I was doing. I knew what would happen if it was found out. I chose. So how can it be your fault?"

Dick's voice was rough. It cut Christina. She felt a tremor go through her. Dick saw her lip quiver, and said desperately, "Christina, you should not have come here."

At that moment a woman's voice called through from the back room: "Dick, who is it?"

Dick muttered softly and went into the room. Christina swallowed hard. She felt completely out of her depth.

Dick came back and jerked his head toward the inner door.
"If you like, you can go and have a word with my mother.
She gets very lonely."

Christina was grateful for the voice that had buffered her
from Dick's harshness. She went eagerly into the back room,
away from Dick's anger, and found herself confronted by a
curious, lively face, startlingly like Dick's, staring at her from
a mound of pillows at the head of the bed. The bed took up
most of the room, covered with tattered blankets and a quilt
of knitted patches; there were a chair and a table, and a fire
burned in the grate, so that the small room was very warm.

"Miss Christina?"

Dick's mother had the same blond hair as Dick, but hers
was grayed and dull with ill health. She had once had Violet's
prettiness, but now she was wasted and gaunt, her eyes set in
hollow sockets. She looked more sixty than forty. Yet, when
she smiled at Christina, there was nothing of resentment or
self-pity in her face.

"Did Dick say Miss Christina? Are you Miss Christina?"

"Yes."

"Oh, I'm glad to meet you! I've heard so much about you!
The children tell me things—I ask them, you see. I like to
know about what's happening, else there is nothing to think
about. Dick has told me what a splendid young rider you are."

She was so genuinely happy to be speaking to her, that
Christina was filled with shame and confusion. Shame that
she had never found out until a day or two previously that
this woman even existed, and confusion to think that she
could be a subject of conversation between Dick and his
mother. Still shattered by her brush with Dick, and now har-
rowed by the plight of his mother, she could not begin to make
a smooth conversation. She felt overwhelmed by the experience
she had let herself in for, and deeply ashamed of her own
ignorance.

Fortunately, Dick's mother was glad of an opportunity to
talk, and Christina, nodding and trying to smile, was able to
gather her wits together gradually. Dick put his head around

the door to say he was going for some water, and when he
had gone Christina was able to explain why she had come.

"I wondered if there was anything I could do, because Dick
is still out of work—it must be very difficult . . ." She found
it hard to say, groping for words.

"I am worried about Dick," his mother said, the animation
dying out of her face. "He is used to working hard, and now
he seems—I don't know—he is very quiet. I don't know how to
explain it. He is always quiet, but not like this. I keep telling
him he will soon get a job, with the crops to lift, if nothing
else, but—" She gave a short sigh, and smiled. "He is very
good to me, you know. He is a far better nurse than Violet,
very gentle. Violet has no patience like Dick. And just now,
she is being rather troublesome. She works hard, I know,
but she keeps telling Dick how hard she is working—it is not
very kind. How tired she is, and he does the cooking and the
chores, and Violet gives him her money, and she—she does
not understand, Miss Christina. She riles Dick, and Dick—
he's one of those quiet ones, he doesn't say anything, but
sometimes I think to myself, these quiet ones—they surprise
you sometimes. When they do break out. I wish she had more
sense. Of course, for a young girl—she does not get much
fun. It is hard."

Christina could say nothing. It was like being beaten inside.

"And if it was not for Dick, what he does, we would be
in trouble. He goes out every night—I should not tell you
this, but I know it is all right with you—and brings something back, a rabbit or a pheasant. It is dangerous, I know,
but otherwise we could not live on what Violet brings. If
he was caught—well, it would be his second offense, and we
could not pay a fine. He would go to prison, I dare say. It is
a great worry, you see. I sometimes think how much easier
it would be for them if I was dead."

She stated a fact, without any self-pity. Christina, listening,
thought of the stables at Flambards, where the sick horses
were given eggs and brandy, and the walls kept out the damp,
the air was warm and fresh and everything shone. She thought

of the new blanket on Goldwillow that Dick had smoothed
the last time she had seen him in the stable: thick and bright
with stripes of black and red on deep yellow. The blankets
she looked at now were gray and threadbare. Dick's mother
was less than a Flambards horse. Dick had always known it.
It was a part of his reserve, his quietness, knowing things like
that, she thought. She could say nothing.

"But there." Dick's mother smiled. "These things have a
way of working out, Miss Christina. I don't want you to think
we spend all our time worrying. People are very kind. The
people next door look after me when the children are away.
Mind you, they've none too much themselves, but they'll always see I'm all right."

She went on talking cheerfully, about the new baby next
door, and Christina smiled and nodded. She felt that her real
self was not in the room at all.

When Dick came back, she got up to go. He stood in the
doorway, not saying anything, and Dick's mother said, "It's
been a real pleasure to meet you, Miss Christina. I hope I
didn't bore you with my talk. I know I talk too much when
I get a visitor. Nobody else gets a chance."

"I have enjoyed it," Christina lied, smiling. She followed
Dick to the front door, and stepped out into the rank garden.
There was nothing they could say to each other. Christina,
learning, did not blunder this time.

"Good-bye, Dick."

"Good-bye, Miss Christina."

William said, "I told you you shouldn't have gone."

"Did you know it was like that?"

"I guessed. I knew about their circumstances. Dick's being
out of work is bound to make life terribly difficult for them."

"But, William, it was awful. The cottage is dreadful. And—
Dick was different. He was angry."

"That doesn't surprise me either. Nobody likes to be caught
at a disadvantage. Cooking the supper, for example. He must
have felt humiliated. You, of all people."

"What do you mean? Me, of all people?"

"Oh, Christina, are you stupid? I don't know much about these things, believe me, but surely it is obvious? That Dick is in love with you? If you don't know, you must be the only one."

Christina stared.

William went on, "You've only got to see the way he looks at you. And what he did for you. He's old enough for all that sort of stuff—eighteen . . . nineteen. That's why I'm so sorry for him, on top of everything. This week or two he must have been getting used to not seeing you, just nicely, and then you have to go and turn up, large as life, on his very own doorstep. It wasn't tactful."

Christina was almost speechless.

"You—you—are making it up!"

And yet, now that William had said it, she saw that it was true. Her instinct had told her that it mattered to Dick very much, the night she had met him in the stables. Yet her everyday self had dismissed it, because he was just a groom. Her everyday self, prosaic, knowing the rules, knew that she could not fall in love with a groom, and she had obeyed the rules. Yet she knew, and had always known that, in a very real way, she did love Dick. Not as he loved her, perhaps, but as well as she had ever known how to love anybody, so far. Why else did his plight matter so much? She dropped her eyes, unable to meet William's fatherly glance.

"Sometimes you are a bit slow, Christina."

She glowered at him. "I thought—I thought . . . Oh!" She was annoyed, out of her depth again. She did not know what she thought. She did not seem to be able to control events any longer. But underneath it all, there was a warmth at knowing Dick loved her.

"I like Dick very much," she said, stating facts. "Better than Mark."

"What has Mark got to do with it?"

Always, at the back of her mind, ever since Aunt Grace's letter, Mark had had very much to do with it. Only as she

spoke did it occur to Christina that William was hardly to
know how her train of thought was moving. But as it was
obviously a day for revelations, she said, "Aunt Grace said that
Uncle Russell was taking me so that Flambards could be
propped up by my money. She said Mark would marry me for
the money."

If Christina had been surprised at William's news for her,
it was as nothing to William's astonishment at her statement.
His jaw dropped.

"What money? Whatever do you mean?"

"When I'm twenty-one, I shall have all the money from
my father's family. I shall be rich." For the very first time in
her life, the thought gave her a sudden pleasure. She was
growing up—the fact had just been proven to her, and twenty-
one was no longer very far away. Six years away. "Aunt Grace
said there was no other reason for Uncle Russell offering to
take me." Then, to be honest, she added, "At least, she didn't
tell me so. She wrote it in a letter and I read it when she
was out of the room. So I suppose I'm not really supposed
to know this."

William was still looking thunderstruck.

"I didn't know! I thought he just wanted a female around
to wait on him as he got older, when Mother went. But if
that's true—"

"Well, it's only Aunt Grace's guessing, I suppose," Christina said hastily. "He didn't tell her that."

"But doesn't it fit in?" William said, suddenly and savagely.
"Oh, it's just his sort of an idea! Aunt Grace is right, I'm
sure of it. Holy Moses! It all fits like a glove! I wonder if
Mark knows about it?"

"Don't tell Mark," Christina said urgently. "Or ask him. I
don't mind your knowing, but it would be awful saying anything to him. He probably doesn't know." She felt acutely
embarrassed at the thought of Mark finding out that he was
expected to marry her.

"Oh, it is all in character!" William was fuming, shocked
and angry.

"It doesn't matter," Christina said, remembering Dick. "It's not for ages, to worry about. Please don't say anything to Mark."

"No."

Christina wondered why, when she was an heiress, she had to be so utterly penniless for all the years before twenty-one. The point was brought home to her immediately. She decided to give Violet some eggs to take home to her mother, but when she had fetched them out of the pantry and wrapped them up, Violet demurred.

"Please, Miss Christina, you must tell Mary, else she might think I've stolen them."

Christina told Mary, who said, horrified, "But if you give those eggs to Violet, what am I going to use all the week? Mr. Russell gives me barely enough for food as it is without me making presents of it, and then he expects to live like a king. Miss Christina, I can't do it. If you want to give eggs away, you must ask your uncle for the money to buy them."

But Christina did not dare to ask him. She had no pocket money, but he bought her riding clothes and horses and paid her hunting license fee. She had food and a room and a home. She could not bring herself to beg for money. She went down to the stable and found eggs in a box in the feed room. She took six and told Fowler.

"Miss Christina," he said, "you can take those now, but don't make a habit of it, else I shall have to answer for them out of my own pocket. Mr. Mark accounts for all the horse-feed bills, and passes them on to Mr. Russell. I don't want to go the same way as Dick."

Christina hurried back to the house, shattered by the knowledge that she had no power at all to help Dick, even in the matter of an egg for his mother. She gave the hard-won gift to Violet, who accepted it rather ungraciously, and with obvious astonishment. The astonishment humbled Christina.

"I have never lifted a finger to help them before today," she realized painfully. "I am no better than Uncle Russell."

Dick Comes Back

"We have a new engine in her now, a twenty-four horsepower Gnome. This has improved our power to weight ratio enormously—she really gets off the ground now, Christina."

"Oh," said Christina.

"We'll show you," William said, grinning. "You don't believe me?"

Christina shrugged anxiously. William's enthusiasm had grown with *Emma's* improvement; Christina had listened, rambling through the summer woods toward Mr. Dermot's establishment, to William's dissertations on the problems of power. Apparently, if the engine was powerful enough to get the aircraft off the ground, it was too heavy for the delicate craft to sustain flight. The new engine had arrived from France, and been installed with reverent precision by *Emma's* guardians.

"Why, if Mr. Blériot has flown the Channel, can't you get *Emma* off the ground?" Christina asked.

"Very few British planes have got up yet," William explained. "All the machines flying in this country are French: Blériots, Voisins, Farmans. Or American variations of the Wrights. There's Mr. Cody—but then he's an American really, although he has just been naturalized. Hardly any British flyer has got a British machine flying. That's the thing—the machine. There's not much satisfaction in just flying what someone else has built."

148

"Oh," said Christina again.

She worried about William now. It was dangerous, she thought, for it all to matter so much. William, at home, hardly spoke; he was in a shining dream, utterly self-contained. But on the way to Mr. Dermot's he talked, to make up for his silence at home. Christina knew about the all important power to weight ratio, the conflicting problems of drag and thrust, and weight and lift, the theories on stability, the subtleties of propeller pitch. She knew that it was William who was going to fly *Emma*, for Joe and Jack were mechanics but had none of William's visionary courage, and Mr. Dermot was too badly handicapped by his short sight.

So when William offered to demonstrate to her *Emma's* new capabilities, she went to Mr. Dermot with mixed feelings. Nervous about the whole business, she was at least glad to be diverted from her preoccupation with Dick's trouble. The optimism at Mr. Dermot's was infectious, and when she stood beside Mr. Dermot outside *Emma's* shed, and watched the strange machine, like an enlarged insect, trundled out into the open, she could not help but catch the excitement herself. William climbed into the precarious seat and tried out the steering controls, while Mr. Dermot talked to Christina about "vertical and horizontal rudders" and Joe and Jack checked on gasoline and oil. William, Christina noticed, had merely a stick in his hand, which when he moved it, caused flaps on the wings to move up and down. With his feet he could move a bar which, with a grinding and revolving of cogs and wires, turned part of the vertical tail from side to side. "Just like a boat," Mr. Dermot said. "For turning to left or right." With his stiff leg Christina could see that moving this rudder bar was very awkward for William, in spite of an extra parallel piece having been fixed on forward especially to accommodate it.

"All right?" Mr. Dermot said.

William nodded.

Jack went round to the tail to hold on, and Joe, seizing the propeller blade, swung it down to start up the engine. This, repeated several times, eventually brought forth a shattering roar and grins of delight all around. Then, after some shouted conversation over the din, William opened out the throttle, and the flimsy machine started to move forward, Jack still holding the tail, and Joe and Mr. Dermot hurrying alongside, one by either wing tip. Caught up in the general excitement, Christina started to run behind, wrinkling her nose at the smell of burning castor oil and the breeze that whirled in her hair. The ground was rough and she saw the little machine bounce, roaring. Jack had dropped off the tail and Joe and Mr. Dermot could no longer keep up, but they all went on running, their eyes riveted on *Emma*, as if drawn by her antics, as she plunged headlong across the rough grass with William perched like a jockey on her slender frames.

Christina, gasping, thought of his being scared on Wood-pigeon, and wanted to laugh. Her eyes were watering. She stumbled and almost fell. When she looked up she saw that *Emma* was off the ground, flying fast and straight at about head level, skimming toward the distant trees with the sun shining through her transparent wings. Christina was shocked by the transition—incredulous. She stood with her hands up to her face, tense with anticipation. She heard Joe say, half jocularly, "At this rate, Mr. Dermot, we're going to have to cut a gap in those trees."

"It's all right," Jack said. "She's coming down."

They all started to run again, as the little craft tilted toward the ground. She tilted too steeply, nosed up again and swayed alarmingly. Then one wing tip dipped; she wobbled, straightened, and hit the ground with a sickening splintering of breaking wood, slithering for some yards in a shower of flying turf.

"The undercarriage again!" Mr. Dermot cried, and they all galloped off to the scene of the disaster. Christina, lifting up her skirts, ran with them, not knowing whether to laugh or cry. William was climbing out, wrinkling his nose with disgust.

"I thought the wing was going to dig in," he said.

"Could be a lot worse," Joe was saying. "It's only the under-carriage, and one prop blade."

"Oh, yes." Mr. Dermot sounded perfectly satisfied. "We can soon fix that."

"If it weren't for the trees, I'm sure she'd climb now," William said. "Or perhaps I could try her the other way, and get out between the house and the big fir tree."

"The incline won't help that way," Mr. Dermot said. "I think Joe is right—we'll cut a gap down the bottom there."

William turned around to Christina and grinned. "Not very spectacular, I'm afraid, but you'll admit she flew?"

"Oh, yes."

"It often ends like this. Sometimes I get her down all right. Once I turned a complete somersault on one wing, and she took a week to put right after that."

Christina did not know what to say. This extraordinary performance was obviously commonplace, the temperamental craft careering along with all her keepers running behind, anxious to assess the amount of damage incurred by this one outing. She did not know whether it was something to admire, or pity.

"Is this what they all do—Mr. Blériot and Mr. Cody? I thought flying was—well . . . higher," Christina finished lamely.

"You wait till we move some trees," William said firmly. "You will see. They all started like this, even the Wright brothers."

Christina did not terribly want to wait and see, for the thought of William. flying over the trees on that frail craft of sticks and oiled silk scared her immeasurably. Yet the whole business was out of her hands; she knew she could say nothing to dissuade William, so did not waste her breath in trying. It was as irrevocable a course as the miserable deterioration of Dick's fortunes.

In June, Christina learned that Dick had left home. Nobody knew where he had gone to, not even Violet. There was a rumor that he had joined the army. The thought of gentle Dick joining the ranks of His Majesty's fighting services made Christina shudder.

"Please tell me if you hear from him," Christina said to Violet.

"Yes, miss," Violet replied demurely. There was a sly look in her eyes that Christina disliked.

Christina knew she should visit Violet's mother, but the memories of the other meeting were so painful she could not bring herself to go. She sent as much as she could with Violet, in the way of food, or a discarded garment, but did no more. Her conscience still hurt her, and she went to Mr. Dermot's more to distract herself that summer, than to enjoy seeing the progress made with *Emma*. For she could not pretend that she enjoyed it.

"Oh, I know I should not let him do it, but he is made for flying!" Mr. Dermot's fanaticism matched William's own. Over and over again he patched *Emma*, and modified her, rebuilt her undercarriage, her tail-rudder, improved her steering mechanism, so that by the time the trees at the bottom of the airfield (now with a large gap in the middle) began to show an autumn yellowing, *Emma* and William were triumphantly soaring above them.

Christina watched, feeling as if her heart were in her throat. The rough, unnatural din of the rotary engine shattered the still sky. The biplane climbed laboriously over the trees, swaying slightly, the small black figure that was William looking anxiously down at his clearance. He could now fly in large circles, banking without losing his equilibrium, and had learned to land, after a series of spectacular swoops and hair-raising near misses. He had crashed several times from the height of a few feet, damaging *Emma* but never himself.

"He has an instinct for it," Mr. Dermot said, watching. "It is like riding a knife edge, flying *Emma*. She needs more stability, to be safe. But William learns fast, he has the feel. It is a gift. We have all tried her, Joe and Jack and myself, and we cannot fly her as William does. There is so little margin for mistakes in these craft, you see. Even taking off, you must judge it just right—there is only just enough power, handling her perfectly. Climbing has to be judged to a degree, not to

lose air speed. Oh, it is tricky, Christina! But look at her!
Worth it, eh? In a few years, who knows what we shall be
seeing?"

He was just like William, Christina thought. They lived in
a world of their own. With its frightening, intermittent roar
the spidery machine passed over their heads, about sixty feet
up. With its big bicycle wheels straddled, its skeletal fuselage
and transparent wings braced with screaming wires, it turned
slowly, painfully, in a careful arc, wobbling occasionally (so
that Christina wanted to shut her eyes), losing height im-
perceptibly. Mr. Dermot started to walk, staring upward.
Slowly, with a heart-stopping coughing of the motor, *Emma*
put down her nose and came across the grass in a shallow
glide, William looking down intently. At the exact moment he
leveled off; *Emma's* nose lifted and her wheels touched,
bounced. The engine gave a last roar, and the machine rolled
across the rough grass, her undercarriage perceptibly groaning, her skids skating over the tufts.

Christina watched the men run forward, all smiling, and
William got down and they started to discuss something.
Christina pushed back her hair, feeling a little shaky. She admired what William was doing enormously, but she could not
become a part of it. She watched him pushing back his cap
with an oily hand, frowning over something in the engine
that Joe was attacking with a wrench. He had grown up, fast.
He was not an enthusiastic little boy, but a man with a job to
do, besides which nothing else mattered. In ten minutes, after
some tinkering with the engine, he was taking off again, and
Christina was watching all over again, her emotions no less agi-
tated.

In spite of William's achievements, in spite of the tragedy
of Dick, life at Flambards continued on its course completely
unchanged and Christina began to look forward to another
season's hunting. She started to ride out with Mark, getting
the grass-fat off their rested hunters, glad of a job to do. Soon
there was fox-cub hunting, and rides through the baring wood-

lands, early, the autumn mist like smoke and the pheasants
rocketing under the horse's hoofs. Mark had his eighteenth
birthday, and said, "This year, I am going to win the Open
on Treasure." And as an afterthought, he added, "And this
year, you can come to the Hunt Ball with me." Christina said
nothing, and felt nothing, neither wanting to, nor not wanting to. Aunt Grace's prophecy nudged her, but it meant nothing. "There is plenty of time for all that," she thought, remembering Dick. And Violet.

Mr. Lucas brought hounds to Flambards for the opening
meet. Christina put her hair up, helped by Mary and a bat-
tery of hairpins, and rode out on Cherry, feeling excited and
confident. In spite of William, the sight of hounds and the
feel of the big horse beneath her made her feel absurdly happy.
Seeing Mark in his hunting scarlet again, on the magnificent
Goldwillow, she forgot all the doubts and uncertainties of the
summer; everything, at that moment, was right. "I am a hunting Russell," she thought, "for sure. William cannot change
it." For once, Russell himself was seeing hounds, sitting in a
chair which Mary had fetched for him in the porch, talking to
Mr. Lucas. Mary and Violet were taking drinks around on
trays. Christina saw Violet cross over to Mark and hold a
glass up for him. Mark leaned down from the saddle, smiling,
and said something to her softly, so that Violet dropped her
eyes and flushed. Christina realized that Mark's broken nose
had done nothing, after all, to spoil his looks, and she was
glad when at that moment Mr. Lucas decided to gather
hounds together with his horn. Mark had to rein back promptly
to make way for Buckle the huntsman, as they moved off.
Christina moved Cherry up beside him, and Mark grinned at
her, and said, "You can have Goldwillow next week, if you
want, when I take Treasure for first horse."

The horses went off in a big bunch, their riders thigh to
thigh and struggling to hold them. The clatter of their hoofs
on the road, and the great sweaty mass of them, all heated up
and excited, barging for place, their riders swearing, quickened
Christina's pulse. She could barge with the best of them, and

swear too, if necessary. Cherry was like a dancing wave beneath her, the big iron shoes striking sparks.

She did not think to look back, otherwise she would have seen Russell struggle up from his chair to lean heavily against the frame of the porch, watching them out of sight. He went on standing there, even when they were gone.

"The old hounds remember me," he said to Violet as she collected up the glasses. Violet gave him a doubtful look. When she had gone, he got his crutches and went back to his seat by the fire, where he drank a lot of brandy, and cried a little, before he fell asleep.

Two months later Christina went into the kitchen and found Violet in floods of tears. She sat at the table with her head buried in her arms, convulsed with sobs, while Mary stood over her, a grim look on her face.

"Whatever's the matter?" Christina said, in amazement.

"With all due respect, Miss Christina, it has nothing to do with you," Mary said shortly.

"Oh." Christina did not inquire any further, until, a week later, Violet was replaced by another girl. Christina, surprised by the new face, said to Mary, "What has happened to Violet?"

"She has left," Mary said abruptly.

"But why? Of her own accord?"

"She was sent away, Miss Christina, and good riddance if you ask me. She was a naughty, wicked girl, and we don't want the likes of her here."

Christina was baffled. "But why? What has she done?"

"Don't ask me, Miss Christina. I don't want to talk about it."

Christina, worried, found William in his room, and said, "What's Violet done?"

William, writing up his diary, said cautiously, "Why don't you ask Mary? She knows more about these things than I do."

"She won't tell me."

"Oh." William went on writing, but he looked worried.

"You know. Why don't you tell me? What's the great mystery?" Christina said, annoyed.

William looked up doubtfully. "She—she is going to have a baby."

Christina gasped. She felt as if the floor had opened up under her feet.

"But how—how can she?"

"What do you mean? How can she?" William was looking embarrassed.

"I mean, she's not married. It's impossible."

William looked hard at Christina, a deep color flushing his cheeks. "Don't ask me about such things. I am not the person to tell you. Only it *is* possible."

Christina felt the color mounting in her own cheeks, because of William's awkwardness. The familiar tide of feelings —of confusion, ignorance, and shock—washed over her, steeping her in mounting embarrassment and distress. She did not know what to believe. She turned away from William, and looked out of the window. If William would not enlighten her, she knew there was nobody else to turn to, that she would never know more than the slender facts she had uncovered. Yet none of it made sense to her. How could such a thing happen?

"Are you sure?"

"Yes." William spoke crossly, with his back to her, leafing through his diary again.

"Does she want one?"

"Oh, for heaven's sake, Christina! I should think it's highly unlikely. Leave me alone."

Christina went to her own room, and looked out of the window there. First Dick, she thought, picking at loose flakes of paint on the sill, now Violet. If Violet had a baby to look after, how was she going to earn any money? She remembered Violet's tears, and knew that Violet's trouble must be as bad as Dick's ever was. The only consolation she had was that, this time, it was no fault of hers.

She went down to the study and wrote a letter to Aunt

Grace, asking her for some money. "It is not for me," she
wrote, "but to help someone I know who is in trouble. It
will be strictly a loan, which I will pay you back, dear Aunt
Grace, when I am twenty-one."

A week later, she received five pounds in the post. Aunt
Grace wrote, "It is all I can spare just now, and I send it in
the hope that the recipient of your kind thoughts will use
it wisely. I only send it because I believe you are a sensible
child, and that I can trust you. But please do not make a
habit of asking for advances on your inheritance, Christina,
as you understand I cannot touch the money and I am only
able to send you money out of my own pocket, loan or no
loan. If you send me your measurements, dear, I will put in
hand your spring undergarments . . ."

Christina, not wishing to repeat her mistake of visiting the
tumbledown cottage in the village, sent the money by post,
with a covering letter. But the letter was returned the next
day, with the envelope marked, "Gone away."

Fowler confirmed that the cottage was empty, and up for
rent.

On Boxing Day hounds put up an old dog-fox that Mr.
Lucas had been swearing vengeance on for two seasons, and
the ensuing run was the best of the winter. When the old
fox was eventually marked down by a stopped earth late in
the afternoon, Mark and Christina were some twelve miles
from Flambards. A bitter rain drove across snow-streaked fields;
the horses steamed and rattled their bits wearily. Mark and
Christina rode the first miles home with Mr. Lucas and the
hunt servants, then he turned off for the kennels, the pack
swirling after him, and they continued along the road for
Flambards together, heads down, weary, seeing little but the
somber flush of sunset shining in the puddles under the
horses' hoofs. They were content, in a manner they had become accustomed to, a mixture of weary satisfaction and the
prospect of Mary's dinner, the day's excitement passed, the
savoring to come. They did not speak but sat down in their

saddles to the slow rhythmic trotting. As they got near Flambards the horses would quicken, but Mark and Christina would
pull them to a walk, to take them home cool. Mark had never
bothered to do this until Christina had scathingly condemned
his bad habits.

The gravel scrunched beneath them as they turned in at
the gates. Treasure, suddenly, stopped dead and gave a whinny,
deep in his throat.

"Get on, idiot horse," Mark said, surprised, giving him a
dig with his spur.

Treasure started, his ears pricked up, excited. Christina saw
somebody step out from the shadow of the fir trees beside
the drive, and reined Drummer in sharply. For an unaccountable reason, she felt a stab of fear go through her.

"Who is it?"

Mark reined Treasure to a halt and said roughly, "What
do you want?"

The figure stepped out on to the drive and stood facing
Treasure. It was a man in khaki uniform. Immediately, Christina understood Treasure's excitement.

"Dick!"

"What do you want?" Mark said again, menacingly. He
shifted the reins in his hands, and shook out the thong of
his hunting whip. Dick came forward, not glancing at Christina, his eyes steady on Mark's face. He did not answer
Mark's question. Christina saw Mark bring up his whip, and
knew instantly that the situation was already out of hand.

Mark lifted his whip and brought the thong down with a
vicious crack. Dick put up an arm, saving his face, and almost
in the same movement lunged forward and caught the stock
of the whip in his hand. With a quick jerk he surprised
Mark, pulling him half out of the saddle; with his other hand
he flung up a wild blow, catching Mark on the side of the
jaw. Treasure bounded forward, frightened by this violence,
and Mark fell heavily backward. Almost before he had hit the
ground, Dick had thrown himself on top of him. He pinned
Mark sharply with a knee to his stomach and hit him again

on the side of the jaw with all the force of his large right hand. Then he caught Mark's collar, lifted him up and hit him again, hard enough to split the black eyebrow with a thick leap of blood.

Petrified with horror, Christina reined in the frightened Drummer and screamed at Dick, "Stop it! Stop it!"

Dick, ignoring her, paused only to let Mark thresh over onto his side and lift himself on one elbow, spitting blood, then he caught him by the back of his coat collar, jerked his head back and hit him again. Driven by an animal instinct for self-preservation, Mark struggled against Dick, rolling over out of the way, but Dick's strength and purpose were utterly merciless. Christina was reminded of a great cat with a mouse. His blond head gleamed in the dusk, the unfamiliar khaki

stretched up over the flexing of his shoulders as he rained
blows on Mark's body. Mark doubled up, crying out, his legs
threshing the grass so that his spurs bit up the clods.

As Drummer pivoted beneath her, scared by something he
did not understand, Christina sobbed out, "Dick! Dick, stop
it! You'll kill him!" But her words were useless. Seeing the
futility of it, she caught Drummer up, and spurred him for
home.

"Fowler will stop him!" she decided. Treasure had already
made for the yard, and when Drummer pounded through
the gates Christina saw Fowler standing there holding him,
with two of the lads gathered anxiously around.

"What's wrong, Miss Christina? Is Mr. Mark all right?"
Fowler reached up for Drummer's reins, his old face crinkled
with alarm.

"Please, Mr. Fowler, stop them! Dick's killing him! They're
fighting, down the drive. Please go and stop them!"

"What, miss?"

"Dick is killing Mark, I'm sure of it! Oh, please—"

"Dick? You mean our Dick, that worked here?"

"Yes. He was waiting for us. He pulled Mark off, and now
he's hitting him—he's like a madman—"

To her utter astonishment, Fowler stepped back, smiling.

"It's not for me to interfere, miss. That's a business between the two lads."

"But you haven't seen them! It's horrible . . . it's insane!
Someone must stop it."

Still on Drummer, she looked at the head groom and the
two boys. They stood in a line between her and the gateway, all smiling. She bit her lips, fighting not to cry in front
of them.

"It's natural, miss, for some things between young men to
be decided this way. It would not be our place to stop it,"
Fowler said.

"But why?" Christina burst out. "Why? What is it all for?"

"Probably Dick has only just heard about Miss Violet, miss,"

Fowler said. "Now don't you bother your head about it. It's none of our concern. They're grown men now, and can look after themselves. I think it would be a good thing if you saw to Drummer yourself tonight, miss. Take your mind off it. You don't want to go up to the house telling your uncle all this now, do you? Let things alone, Miss Christina. Come along. Let Drummer have a bit of a drink now, only a little, mind."

He was talking to her as he used to when she first learned to ride, as if she were just a little girl. Christina's head whirled. She realized that she felt very tired and when she at last got down off Drummer her legs trembled beneath her. She tried to understand the implications of Fowler's words. She led Drummer into his box and slipped off his bridle, his saddle, fastened him up by his headcollar. One of the boys brought him a bucket of gruel, and as the horse sank his head into the bucket, Christina leaned her head on his damp back, the words falling over themselves in her head, seeing Mark's face pummeled by Dick's fist, the blood breaking out, and Dick's ruthless face contorted with anger, hearing the animal grunts and gasps. And the things Fowler had said, which did not make sense to her unless . . .

"How can I tell? How do you know things, when nobody explains?" she wept to Drummer, burying her face into the coarse blackness of his mane. There was nobody in the world to Christina just then, as she stood there in Drummer's warmth, aware of her terrible ignorance. The boys' grins . . . old Fowler's satisfaction . . . even William . . . among them all, there was nobody, nobody whom she could speak to, who understood the black cage of her loneliness. Only once, in this very same spot, had it been different, when Dick had put his arms around her. The old Dick. Now Dick was changed too. Christina bit back a hiccup of self-pity, and pulled Drummer's rugs over his back, her skirt rustling the thick straw. Fowler was right, that she should see to Drummer, in the calm orderliness of the stables, hide herself in the sweet-smell-

ing dusk while the doubts and emotions pulled at her. "Why
are they so cruel to each other?" she thought. Everyone in
Flambards hurting each other . . .

"Drummer all right, Miss Christina?" Fowler asked.

Christina blew her nose. "Yes, thank you."

"I'll see to him now."

"Thank you."

"You go straight into the house now. Don't worry about
those lads. It's never as bad as it looks."

Christina hesitated. "What shall I tell Mr. Russell?"

"The truth wouldn't hurt," Fowler said. He put a fatherly
hand on her shoulder. "Go on. Don't be afraid. This is something the old man will understand. He was a one with his
fists once, Miss Christina. He'll laugh."

Fowler was quite right. Russell laughed. He tried to draw
Christina out about the day's sport, but she would not speak
to him, conscious of Mark's empty place across the table. William ate in silence. Christina kept her eyes on her plate.
She was very tired, and the warmth sapped what little energy
she had left. The candle flames blurred before her eyes. When
they had finished the meal, she said to Russell, "Please, will
you excuse me?"

He nodded, and Christina went upstairs to look for Mark.
Perhaps he would not want to see her; perhaps Dick had left
him in no fit state to drag himself home. Doubtfully Christina knocked at the door of his room. There was no reply.
Christina turned the knob and went in.

"Mark?"

The room was in darkness, but Mark lay in a huddle on the
bed, still in his jacket and boots. He was barely conscious,
his breath coming in painful snores. Her weariness needled
by anxiety, Christina lit the candles and went over to him.

"Mark, are you all right? It's me, Christina."

She put the candles down and bent over him. He lay with
his head on the pillow, which was dark with blood. His eyes
were closed with swellings, his nose flattened and cut. If
Christina had not known it was Mark, there was nothing there

that she would have recognized, from the blood-slicked hair on his sweating forehead to the split, swollen lips, painfully parted for breath, the teeth showing broken between. His stock was torn off, his scarlet jacket split in ribbons. Christina looked at him, biting her lips. She expected to feel horror, and she felt only a dispassionate anger. She felt as old as Aunt Grace. This was a laughing matter, she remembered (according to Fowler and Russell), natural to young men. Dick, her own gentle Dick, had been roused to do this dreadful damage. "Men are so stupid," she thought, and her pity was as much for Dick as it was for Mark. She leaned over and pushed Mark's hair back gently from the battered face.

"Christina." Mark spoke with difficulty. His hand came up, groping for hers. The icy fingers, strong enough to hold Treasure, held hers compulsively. "Stay with me."

PART THREE: *1912*

The Point-to-Point Race
Interrupted

Christina had ridden to the point-to-point course on Woodpigeon, and now wished she had driven over in the carriage,
for with Fowler seeing to Treasure, and Mark in the paddock,
there was no one to take Woodpigeon. She would have to
sit on him till Mark's race was over. Not that she minded
really: the women in the paddock were smart in their bespoke
tweeds, and she had nothing but her riding habit that fitted
her to perfection. Aunt Grace had promised her a ball dress
for the Hunt Ball next week, but it had not yet arrived. Christina was not exactly sure whether she wanted it to arrive, for
if it were mislaid she would not have to go, which would solve
many problems.

She leaned forward, stroking Woodpigeon's neck absently.
A year ago, after the last Hunt Ball which she had attended
with Mark and not enjoyed very much, William had asked
her to go to the next one with him.

"With you?" she had said, amazed. "I thought you hated
anything to do with hunting people?"

"Did you enjoy it with Mark?" William asked.

"Not very much. He got drunk."

"Well then, what have you got to lose? I shan't get drunk.
I want you to come with me. A genuine, bona fide offer. Will
you accept?"

"I can't understand you."

"You'll come?"

"Well, yes. I will."

She thought he had asked her just to annoy Mark. Mark did not know about it yet, and Christina wished she had not left it so late, telling him. "It will serve him right for taking me for granted," she thought. "He hasn't troubled to ask me, but just assumed I'm going with him." She knew that he would be terribly annoyed. When Mark was annoyed he was just like his father. She dreaded what sort of a mood he would be in if he did not win this race on Treasure.

He had bet a lot of money on the race, and stood to lose more than his pride if Treasure failed him. The year before he had been second to young Allington's Mayflower. Christina, thinking of his rage, could not help but compare his anger in disappointment to William's stubborn suppression of excitement. For William, the past two years, had had his disappointments as well as the triumphs. Emma's successor had been a failure; Emma Three had been damaged beyond repair when her engine caught fire and William had had to crash-land in a field of turnips—miraculously escaping injury himself—and Emma Four, the current model, had been suffering from a series of teething troubles with a new steering invention that Mr. Dermot was trying out. Now, at eighteen, William's dedication was more complete than it had ever been. Through Mr. Dermot he was trying to get himself a job at the Royal Aircraft Factory at Farnborough; failing that, he had mentioned trying to join the Royal Flying Corps which was just being formed. He no longer cared who knew about his work. Most of the people in the neighborhood knew who sat at the controls of the little biplane that was to be seen occasionally skimming over the trees; Mark knew, but was not much interested, and, if Russell knew, he chose to ignore the matter. William had taken to staying at Mr. Dermot's for several days at a time, and Russell never commented on his disappearance. When he was not at home Christina missed him in a way that surprised her. She felt that Flambards was incomplete.

Woodpigeon shifted, pricking his ears, as the starter's horse came out from the crowd toward him. Christina stroked him again. It struck her, thinking of William, that it was Woodpigeon, in a way, that had set William on his path. If William had had to go on hunting, everything might have turned out differently for him. Woodpigeon, in his middle age, was a quiet lady's horse, a bold hunter still, but without the impetuosity that had led to William's accident.

"Queer," Christina thought, pleased. She liked to see patterns in life, which proved that everything was not quite so inconsequential as sometimes it seemed. She gave Woodpigeon another affectionate pat. Mark did not ride him any more. He preferred Goldwillow and his faithful Treasure.

The runners for the Open were leaving the paddock now. The paddock was just a roped-off circle in the middle of a large field on the side of a hill. The brow of the hill formed a fine vantage point for the course, which lay in a circle around the valley below and up the side of the hill beyond. Christina lifted her head and sniffed the warm April breeze, excited and —suddenly—very happy for everything she was a part of. She felt she belonged here, on the side of the green hill, within sound of the bookies' shouting and the noise of the spectators, the big, handsome horse beneath her and her body easy to his, a part of him, as once she had envied in Dick and Mark when they were just boys. Two sea gulls cried over the hill, white wings flashing.

The horses were moving away to the start, out of the paddock, and their hoofs drummed on the firm turf. The ground was dry, the stream bed fringed with bright, bursting osier buds and white sloe blossom, the red flags showing the horses the way through. The course took them down the trampled bluebell slope and over the water, with a nasty rail on the far side, then up the steep hill beyond and over a thick layered hedge into the lane by Colonel Badstock's rambling Elizabethan house. There they would be out of sight for a couple of hundred yards, and all eyes would be on the flags in the hedge under Badstock's Wood where they would jump into view again. Following the course around with her eyes, Christina could feel herself jumping it, and for a moment quite wished she were Mark. Then she saw his face as he went by to the start, and decided that perhaps it would be no joy ride, not when it meant as much as it did to Mark.

"They were fools to put so much money on it," she thought. Russell had laid fifty pounds on Mark to win. And yet Cherry was up for sale, because Russell said he could not afford to keep so many horses. For the first time since Christina had come to Flambards, economy was hitting the stables. One of the boys had been dismissed and not replaced.

Christina cantered Woodpigeon across the side of the hill and drew him up close behind the starter's horse. The ten runners were circling excitedly, all horses Christina knew, only their riders looking unfamiliar in silks. Treasure, already raking at his bit so that Mark could scarcely hold him, stood out from the others, superbly powerful and fit. Of them all, he was a horse who needed a good rider, to keep his mind on the job, to save his exuberance, merely to hold him on the course. Treasure had never become a lady's ride. He was as hard and as headstrong as Mark. Christina had never ridden him since the day Dick had saved her from the big hedge.

She curbed Woodpigeon's fidgeting and watched Mark. He was white with strain, dark eyes scowling. His features had never recovered from Dick's pounding, for all their having survived over the years the damage of his thrustful riding; his nose was thickened and slightly bent, one eyebrow scarred with a puckered hairless line. When he called across to the starter, confirming his presence, he showed his broken front teeth. There was nothing boyish any longer about his face. It was arrogant and vital. He controlled Flambards now, whether Russell knew it or not, and when she watched him, recognizing his power, Christina could feel afraid, for she knew that her future was in his hands too. She was only seventeen yet, four tricky years to negotiate before she came into her fortune.

The starter had the horses in line, and Treasure was up on the inside, Mark sitting hunched, ready to go with the horse, his fingers clenched to hold him until the white flag fell. Christina could see the reins quivering, Treasure's nostrils opened out red, the hocks gathered up and dancing, a coiled spring for Mark to release with his aching fingers. Young Allington with his red hair and freckles, John Badstock on his father's brown mare Ladybird, and Lucas' nephew Peter on a big chestnut called Firedance stood shoulder to shoulder beside him, all good riders for Mark to watch. "If only," Christina thought, "Mark were more . . ." She groped for a word . . . "clever . . . intelligent—with Treasure, they could not beat him, barring a fall." And she remembered Dick, who had understood Treasure, wasted now looking after a train of stupid mules in some transport regiment in India . . . "Oh, if Dick were here!" Christina thought, conscious suddenly, on Dick's behalf, of the sweet freshness of the April breeze. It had the power to hurt still, as if it had happened yesterday, what she had done to Dick. It stung her, bitterly, even as the horses leaped forward with a convulsed creaking of saddle leather and scoring of fresh turf. The smell of the sweating horses, the smell of clean leather, Woodpigeon raking out in sudden excitement, but so obediently curbed—all of it was so much a part of Dick's life that Christina, even in the heat of the moment, was grieved for his exile.

Treasure got a good start and went down the first field maddened with excitement, a length ahead of all the others. Mark managed by sheer brute strength to steady him for the first fence, a straggly hedge into a sparse covert, and he jumped it big, with a whirl of his black tail and a shower of clods into the faces of the riders behind. The covert was awkward. After the first wild dash the horses had to be caught up and steadied; Christina could make out the vivid yellow of Mark's silks skidding cautiously through the trees. Treasure was cantering like a rocking horse, his nose tucked in, and Mark was bent over him to miss the whipping twigs of the young oaks. Behind him, a gray mare, having lost her rider at the first fence, was galloping on. She bumped Treasure, then balked at the long slippery descent to the stream and ran off

the course, to the relief of the riders behind her. Treasure
went down the hill fast, in a flurry of mud.

"Too fast!" Christina said to herself. She fidgeted with
Woodpigeon's reins, anxious, and the big gray, as if anxious
too, pivoted uneasily, and pawed the ground. Cloud shadows
darkened the hill above Badstock's, but a gleam of sunshine
followed, bursting over the top of the hill to lay a bright
finger of color across the grass. The distances were violet-
sharp, the clouds radiant. The air was warm and heavy with
spring moisture. Christina felt her excitement mounting as
she turned her face to the warm wind and the long hill that
the horses were now climbing. It was a heartbreaking hill,
to find out a fit horse, and Treasure and Firedance climbed it
side by side, with Ladybird and Allington's Mayflower string-
ing out behind. Two horses had fallen at the stream, and the
gray mare had disappeared from view, on a race of her own.

"That should calm Treasure down a bit," Christina thought,
watching Mark take a pull at him for the big hedge out at
the top. Firedance, with a longer stride than the compact
Treasure, had gone ahead, and took the hedge first, hitting
it hard with his forelegs and disappearing in a heap into the
lane. Christina did not expect to see him again, but some-
how young Peter managed to stay on, and they appeared on the
far strip with Peter entwined around the horse's neck, fighting
to regain his seat. Treasure took the fence beautifully, Mark
sitting well back but leaving him plenty of rein.

"At least," Christina thought, warming to Mark's performance, "he doesn't interfere with his mouth, like some of them.
Treasure's never been afraid of jumping. If only Mark will
nurse him a bit when he's getting tired . . ."

Now that the horses had disappeared behind a high hedge
and trees, she felt very nervous, watching and waiting. The
crowd was thickening on the hill, buzzing with a single ex-
pectant voice. Half the county seemed to be in attendance,
drawn by the warm spring weather; below the paddock and
the marquees, rows of farm carts and carriages were drawn
up, the horses taken out of the shafts and tied on behind

with a nosebag for company, where they stood placidly, un-
perturbed by the efforts of their more aristocratic brothers out
on the field. Woodpigeon, patiently shifting legs, pricked his
ears, and gazed out across the hill.

"Is he coming?" Christina murmured. "Where's our old
Treasure then, my beauty?"

She stroked Woodpigeon's white neck, very anxious.

The crowd gave a shout, which sent the sea gulls spiraling in
sudden alarm, and Christina saw Firedance appear with an
enormous leap over Colonel Badstock's five-barred gate out of
the wood. Behind him, side by side, Mayflower and Treasure
jumped together. Christina's throat tightened nervously. The
three horses were all old hands, very evenly matched, and if
none of them fell, it was going to be a very close race. Christina dreaded Mark's anger, if he lost again.

The crowd kept up its eager murmur now, as the three horses
strung out across the fast ridge at the top of the valley, Firedance leading by two lengths. A post and rails went over the
top, built into the high hedge. Firedance rapped it, but without coming to any harm; Treasure flew it very fast, gaining
a length, but Mayflower got underneath it and cracked the

rail in pieces, his rider flying headfirst over the horse's shoulder. The crowd roared. Christina shifted in her saddle.

"Oh, Mark!" she whispered. "You can win, if you want!"

The course turned right, downhill now, back toward the
starting point. There was a big ditch in the valley, the last
fence, then a long uphill run to the finish, which was a dour
test for stamina. There were only Firedance and Treasure in
the race with a chance now, for the three remaining horses
were strung out more than twenty lengths behind, none of
them making any impression on the two leaders. The crowd
on the hill started to chant the two names. At the same
time, above the excited noise, Christina heard another sound,
utterly unexpected but, to her ears, very familiar. She turned
around in her saddle, and to her horror and amazement, saw
the skeletal shape of Emma Four shaving the top of Colonel
Badstock's ornate Elizabethan chimneys, having barely cleared
the surrounding trees, her wings wobbling in an extraordinary
fashion.

Christina knew instantly that there was something wrong,
and that William was obviously in serious trouble. Emma
Four was heading straight across the valley for the hill the
crowd was using for its vantage point; she was flying almost
at stalling speed, and clearly, unless William managed something miraculous, she was not going to weather the summit.
Her engine was making temperamental noises, opening up in
raucous bursts as William tried desperately to gain height, then
conking out in a series of coughs and splutters. Christina could
see William in his flat oily cap and goggles, peering anxiously
over the side. For a moment, the thought crossed her mind
that he had timed his arrival at the run-in on purpose, for
some diabolical reason of his own, but then she realized that
he was a long way past doing anything for any other motive
than that of saving his own skin.

His arrival created immediate havoc. Christina was aware of
it almost as soon as she set eyes on Emma Four by the nervous
plunge beneath her of the calm Woodpigeon. She reined
him in sharply, talked to him soothingly and stroked his neck,

her eyes switching from William to the horses completing the race. Firedance and Treasure had just cleared the big ditch which formed the last obstacle, and were starting neck and neck up the long run-in. The crowd's roar had changed to a frantic, amazed gabble. Christina watched, her eyes widening with a dreadful anticipation, as the harmless afternoon's entertainment suddenly took on an almost comic inevitability. So intimately concerned with the chief participants, she nevertheless felt completely detached, utterly unable to do anything to help either Mark or William at these separate crises of their lives.

The crowd started to run. They ran in all directions, some aimlessly, still watching the stricken *Emma Four*, pointing and gesticulating, some in real, screaming panic. The flying machine came down over the valley, very low, her wings rolling horribly, engine screaming. All the horses tied to the farm carts started to plunge and whinny madly, some breaking away. Christina saw one gallop full tilt into the tea tent by one opening, and out with a frightful crashing noise in its wake through the other. One horse, still between the shafts of a smart gig, bolted down the hill and got stuck in the stream. Firedance and Treasure, one moment galloping toward this monstrous, screaming apparition, were now bolting headlong back down the valley. Firedance ran himself to a standstill, and Peter was able to fling himself off and hold his head, but Treasure, mad with fright, would not stop for the hedge and stream at the bottom and went straight through the obstacle as if it did not exist. Mark was flung violently from the saddle by a blow from a low branch, and fell heavily down the bank below, leaving ribbons of yellow silk speared on the thorn hedge like breaking willow buds. Christina watched the whole sequence from Woodpigeon's back with a sense of doom, utterly calm because there was nothing she could do. She winced for Mark, and turned to watch William make his forced landing, so close to her now that she could see the tense look on his face, the stiff leg stuck out in its awkward fashion in front of him.

She could tell that he had picked the flat spot at the finish
to put *Emma Four* down on, but at the angle he was coming
to it, it was very short, for a hedge ran beyond it, dividing
the grazing on the hill itself. Worse than that, a group of
panic-stricken women chose at the last moment to run in the
wrong direction. Christina bit her lip, drawing blood, as *Emma
Four* roared toward them. Their skirts flew up, revealing white
petticoats and long, stalky legs like the legs of panicking hens
that she had seen running before the de Dion. Christina
clenched her hands on the reins and cried out, "William!"

Emma Four's engine roared. William was too low to turn,
and had no alternative but to put the aeroplane's nose up
and clear the women by flying over them. They had the sense

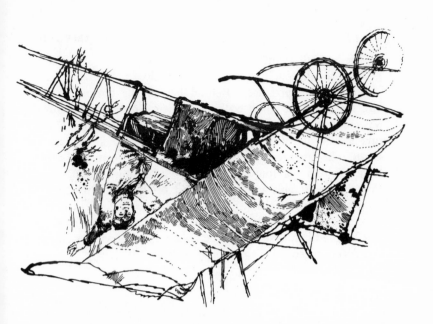

to throw themselves down on the ground (or they fainted with fright, Christina was never sure which) and *Emma Four's* skids went over them with about five feet to spare. It was as if she threw her nose up as a last dying gesture to please, for immediately the engine cut out again and she nosedived sickeningly into the thorn hedge beyond. Her tail cartwheeled, one wing dug in with a sickening rending of cracking timber. Burying her nose deep into the hedge, *Emma Four* then rolled and came to rest upside-down, her undercarriage wheels spinning against the sky.

The scattered crowd now, with a whoop, started to run back in *Emma Four's* direction, babbling and shouting with excitement. But Christina, spurring Woodpigeon with such urgency that he did not think to hesitate, arrived by the stricken aircraft first. She flung herself off the horse and peered into the hedge.

"William!"

William's face, ludicrously surprised, was staring back at her, upside-down. He was still in his seat, suspended by his webbing seat belt.

"Are you all right?"

"Yes, thank you," he said very politely.

Christina stepped back. Behind her, at the bottom of the hill, she could see Mark walking in their direction. The crowd was converging; Woodpigeon pranced in nervous circles. Christina looked at William again. Quite suddenly, she began to laugh. The laughter rose up inside her like a great, uncontrollable explosion, a fountain of irrepressible mirth. She seized Woodpigeon's reins and led him out of the crowd which was now piling up all around, jostling and shoving. When they were clear she leaned against his warm white neck and laughed. She laughed helplessly, until the tears poured down her cheeks, and Woodpigeon, losing interest, started to graze.

William's Promise

"Of course it was funny," Christina said acidly to Mark. "It was the funniest thing I've ever seen. Is laughing forbidden at Flambards?"

Mark glowered. "Of all the damn-fool, idiot exhibitions to make of himself!"

"He didn't do it on purpose, did he?"

"You'd think so, timing it like that! He couldn't have timed it better if he'd planned it for weeks. Just when we had it in the bag! Treasure had Firedance beaten—it was just a matter of cantering up the hill! And then that fool—!"

Christina sighed wearily. Mark had been rampaging all the evening, and she was tired of listening to him. She was in the kitchen, serving up the dinner. Mary had cooked it, and left it in the oven, having taken a rare evening off to visit her aunt. The kitchen, at that moment, was the best place to be, for William had been closeted in the dining room for the last hour and a half with his father, and such was the atmosphere that Christina preferred to stay out of the way. Mark had been in there for an hour, but hunger had eventually overcome his wrath and he had joined Christina in the kitchen to see if any food was forthcoming.

"Go and see if I can take it in to the table," Christina said. "They must have finished now."

179

"Oh, Father could go on for hours yet," Mark said. "He's really into his stride. He didn't know of any of Will's goings-on. It's come as a real shock to the old system."

"Well, if I dish up, it might shorten it a bit. He's had long enough surely? And I'm sure Will has." She straightened up from the fire and pushed back her hair. "The potatoes are done. They'll go to mush if we wait any longer."

"All right. I'll go and warn them."

Mark went out and Christina started to drain the potatoes. A large parcel addressed to her lay on the dresser, where Mary had left it. It was postmarked from London, and she guessed it was her dress for the Hunt Ball. She was dying to open it, but had decided to contain her curiosity until a quieter time. Although at least William was too big now to get beaten, Christina had no doubt that things in Flambards were not going to be quite the same again after this marathon row; the day was going to leave its mark. William, she guessed, would be standing there saying very little, his face closed up with contempt, which would sting Russell to even greater fury. When Russell rowed with Mark, they both shouted, and Christina felt that they even enjoyed it. But with William it was different. It was real, and bitter, and went much deeper than the mere events of a day.

Mark came back grinning.

"All right. Father's getting exhausted, I think. And Will looks as if he could do with a square meal."

"You take something in, too," Christina said.

"I'm not Violet."

"A good thing for you," Christina said quickly. Mark, to her astonishment, colored up, and took the meat pie and went out of the kitchen without another word.

It was difficult pretending that the day had been like any other. Russell looked gray and spent, and drank very heavily. William was pale, and ate little. Only Mark ate heartily, but between courses he resumed his damning of William for depriving him of his race, presumably not having had a chance to say much before Russell had exhausted himself. William did not reply. Only once, when Mark complained about the money he had lost in betting, William said coldly, "I will pay you back."

After dinner Christina cleared the table, and started to wash up in the scullery. The fire glowed in the range, but outside the darkness was warm too, the stars hazy behind warm veils of spring cloud. Christina went out to throw away some rubbish, and saw the overgrown garden rippling and sighing in the dusk, the great cedar breathing its strange foreign scent to the English spring. The remains of a herb garden, seeding itself, pushed up between the cobbles under her feet; gaunt arms of dried angelica rustled against the wall.

"Flambards," Christina said to the house, "you are dying."

The ivy was stifling the doors and windows. Nobody cared. Christina had tried to get a groom to clean up the garden, but Russell would have none of it. She had tried to freshen up the house, but Russell would buy no new carpets or curtains. He would not get the electricity. (Mary had said grimly, "And if it ever comes, it will go to the stables first, mark my words.") Flambards was decaying, with great dignity, ivy-bound, roses rampant, reverted to briar, brown paneling drying and cracking, flagstone breaking up, tiles slipping, chimneys smoking. Christina looked out on the garden, and thought, "Mark does not want it any different, either." There was no future in Flambards.

"Christina? Are you there?"

Christina turned back into the kitchen with a start. William was standing in the doorway.

"What is it? I was putting the rubbish out."

"I just wanted to tell you . . ."

"What? Oh, Will, you've had a wretched time. Is it all right? What's he been saying?"

Christina shut the door behind her and went across to the fire, where William was standing. He was tall now, as tall as Mark, but not nearly so heavy. His face had none of Mark's brutal vitality; it was a kind face, and yet impatient. He could be bitterly angry in a way that made Mark's raging seem trivial, yet he could be compassionate in a way that Mark did not know.

"He says he's going to send me away," William said. "There's a brother of his in British Columbia—he says I can go there and learn forestry. He's sending a telegram off straight away, and one to book my passage."

Christina looked at William, appalled. "You don't mean it? He's just blustering!"

"Oh, he means it all right." William said bitterly. "He can't wait to see me go." He paused, and smiled suddenly. "I shall go away all right, but not to British Columbia."

"Where will you go? If you go to Mr. Dermot—"

"Yes, he will fetch me back, he told me so. He says he will prosecute Mr. Dermot, if I go there again."

"But, Will, you must! You can't give it all up just because of him!"

"What he says doesn't really matter any more." William said. "Only Mr. Dermot mustn't suffer for it. He can send as many telegrams as he likes, but I shall go where I please. I just wanted to tell you, so that you know what's happening."

"Where will you go?"

"Mr. Dermot will lend me some money, and I shall go and get a job—at Farnborough, or Brooklands, or Hendon, or wherever I can—and then I shall pay him back. I shall never come back here again."

Christina, having known that this was going to happen sooner or later, was unprepared for the announcement so soon. She felt almost as if she had received a physical blow. It was not William she grieved for, she told herself instantly, but herself left without him. It was all she could do not to let him see her self-pity.

"It is the best thing," she said firmly. She did not dare say anything else.

"I shan't tell Mark or Father what I'm doing but if they ask, you can tell them. I don't care if they know. I just thought I wouldn't like to leave without telling you, that's all."

"Are you going now?"

"I'll sleep here, and go in the morning."

"Oh."

He was very calm and matter-of-fact, and Christina sat at the table opposite him, and decided to be very calm and matter-of-fact too.

"What about poor *Emma Four*?"

William grinned. "Joe and Jack came up later with the cart and took her home. You know what happened? It was the rudder—Mr. Dermot's new idea. It doesn't work. I couldn't turn the kite—the whole works packed up. And there I was on course for the only real hill for miles, and the old engine started playing up as well. I was looking for somewhere to put her down, but the field behind Badstock's was full of cows. So I weathered that, only to find the next likely spot covered with half the country on their day's jaunt, not to mention tea tents, farm carts and racehorses galloping about all over the place. I was in a rare sweat, I can tell you, because I knew she wouldn't go over the top. And those silly women—phew! I thought I was going to slice their heads off."

"Is *Emma Four* bad?"

"No. Not really. Not as bad as you'd have thought, considering what happened. The engine and the fuselage weren't damaged."

But Christina was not really interested in *Emma Four*. She watched William, keeping her back to the oil lamp. On the dresser she could see the parcel from Aunt Grace with her ball dress in. She would be going with Mark after all. She felt no impatience to open the box any more. It did not seem to matter any longer.

"Well, Christina, now you know, I might as well go and tidy up my things. I'll let you know how I get on. This is probably all for the best."

"Yes."

"Good night then. Good-bye, I suppose." He stood at the door, smiling.

"Good-bye. Good luck, with everything."

"Thank you. And for you. Don't fall off," he said.

When he had gone, Christina sat on in front of the fire. The kitchen was quiet and warm, but Christina was cold, and felt numb in her mind, in a way she had never experienced before. It was as if nothing that she could think of in the future had the power to make her feel either happy or sad. As if nothing mattered any more. Not the dress, nor the ball, nor hunting, nor the point-to-point.

"It's the shock," she thought. "I'll get used to the idea." Flambards, after all, saw very little of William, even when he lived there. It surely would be much the same, Christina thought. But the feeling she had had just now, looking at the garden, that Flambards was decaying, came back again. And now there was no touch of beauty in Flambards' decay, as there had been before, as she stood in the soft dusk. Now Flambards, choked in ivy, hemmed around by its wilderness, seemed to stand for everything that was backward and ignorant. She remembered Mr. Dermot's house, and how she had thought of it as shining. Nothing shone in Flambards. Christina felt that with William's going, she had been abandoned to the backwardness, the wilderness of Flambards. She remembered Dick saying, five years ago, "There's men worked for him, day in, day out, and never had as much pleasure in all their lives as he got in one day before his accident." Why should she remember that?

She got up off the table. Dick's mother had died in the poorhouse a year after Violet had left. Violet had gone to London with her baby and had not been heard of since.

"What is the use of remembering all those things again?" Christina said to herself angrily. There were new things to be sore about, without raking up the old ones.

She turned around and fetched the parcel, and laid it on the table. She cut the string, and opened it, and pulled aside the layers of tissue paper. Aunt Grace's dresses were always very practical, and very well-made, with stout hems, and cuffs that took off for washing. Christina expected even her ball dress to be severely useful, able to last for several seasons. She was totally unprepared for what she found.

The dress was of a deep rose silk, the fashionably slim skirt embroidered all over with tiny crystal beads. The bodice was brief, deeply cut, the neckline trimmed with a fretwork lace of the tiny beads. There were no sleeves, but a stole of pale pink tulle, embroidered with crystal flowers, was folded underneath. There was also a small bag on a gold chain of the same rose-pink silk, a pair of long pink gloves, and a pair of pink silk shoes with silver buckles.

Christina had never seen anything like the dress since she had last peered into Aunt Grace's sewing room six years ago. She had forgotten that women even wore dresses such as this. The dress she had worn last year had been one of her Aunt Isabel's that Mary had roughly altered to fit, with a bow at the back to hide the moth hole. It had been dark green, and Christina had not been convinced that it had not started life as black. Mark, when he was drunk, had told her that she looked as beautiful as his mother, which had prompted Christina to go home.

"But this—!"

Christina held it up, and the skirt slithered heavily to the floor, glittering like a tropical snake. A letter fell out of its folds. Christina picked it up with one hand and held it to the light to read.

Dear Christina,

I trust that the dress will reach you in plenty of time. I do hope it is suitable. I made it for the daughter of a very old client of mine, but the daughter eloped, leaving no address, and her mother returned it, as she did not wish to set eyes on any of her daughter's belongings. The measurements are the same as yours, but if it is too dashing, dear, there is time to let me know and I will send the dark brown crepe that I was intending to let you have. It only needs the fasteners putting on, otherwise is quite ready. I do not know what these Hunt Balls are like these days, but in my day they were dressy affairs, so perhaps this will not be out of place. Do be careful not to drink too much, Christina. It is very unseemly and can get

you into bad trouble. I just mention this because I know that
Russell was always a heavy drinker and no doubt has brought
the boys up to be the same, and you have no one to advise
you. I hope you will enjoy yourself.

Your loving Aunt Grace.

Christina dropped the letter, and held the dress up again. It
was very beautiful, and very useless, she thought. She had no
desire to go to the Hunt Ball any longer, if William was not
going to take her.

But in the morning, when William had left, she found a
note slipped under her bedroom door. It just said, "I will
call for you at 8 p.m. next Saturday. W."

When Russell discovered that William had gone, he sent
Fowler around to Mr. Dermot's. Fowler returned to declare
that William was not there, and that Mr. Dermot did not
know where he was. This satisfied Russell.

"He'll turn up when he can't find a job," he growled. "He'll
come back when he's hungry. And if he doesn't, good riddance
to him."

Christina told Mark, "He's coming back next Saturday, to
take me to the Hunt Ball." It had to be told sooner or later.

"He's what?" Mark turned on her, incredulous.

"He asked me to go to the ball with him, and I said I
would."

"He asked you! But you're coming with me!"

"You never asked me."

"Asked you? But you knew, surely?" Mark was almost too
dumfounded for words.

"How am I supposed to know, if you don't ask me?" Christina said coolly, ready for battle.

"For heaven's sake, Christina! Of course you knew I wanted
to take you. You're not really saying you're going with William? You must be mad! How can he dance, for a start?"

"He couldn't be any worse than you," Christina retorted.

"When did he ask you?"

"Last year."

"Last year! You don't really mean it, do you? That you're going with him?"

"Yes, I do mean it. And if he doesn't call for me, I shall stay at home."

"You must be out of your senses!" Mark was very angry. "If he doesn't call for you, you will certainly stay at home, for I shan't take you now."

In spite of the note, Christina was prepared for William not to come. She did not really believe he would. She would not let herself think that he would, because she did not want to be disappointed. For some reason, it mattered desperately that William should come. Christina was startled by this perverse longing for William, but it was a feeling she had no control over at all. She thought of him all the time, wondering what he was doing, wondering whether he would remember the hasty promise scribbled on the scrap of paper, which she kept in the drawer of her dressing table, and looked at every night when she went to bed. His writing was very adult, refined and quick, not like Mark's thick scrawl. She sat at her dressing table with the paper in her hand, and did not dare to think that he would really bother to come back for such a stupid function.

"He hates that sort of thing. And now he has so much to think about . . . I don't know why he ever asked me in the first place. And if he comes here, Russell will see him, and there will be another great row." There were so many reasons why he shouldn't come, and only the bit of paper to say he would.

Mark, even more angry than she had prepared for at her refusal to go with him, did not speak to her all the week. For Christina it was a long, lonely week. Having by necessity grown self-sufficient, and never—skeptically—allowed herself to indulge in what she called "dreams," Christina now found herself helplessly succumbing to long periods of asinine make-believe of such sentimental unreality that she sometimes wondered if she was going off her head. It was William who featured in these daydreams. William who, Christina reminded herself sharply, cared for nothing at all in life but flying, and who had asked her to the Hunt Ball merely to spite his brother. Christina was experiencing for the first time the unmerciful agonies of being in love with someone who knew nothing about it, and she was utterly bewildered.

"Why? Why?" she asked herself angrily. "Nothing is any different. Nothing is changed. Why should I feel like this?"

It was Mark she was destined to marry, according to Aunt Grace, and the idea had never upset her, until now. It had never made her want to jump with excitement either, she remembered, but it had seemed a logical, convenient idea, belonging to an unreal and distant future which she had thought very little about. "But William wouldn't want to get married, not to anyone," Christina thought. "Least of all to me."

By Friday, the thought of getting dressed for the ball and waiting to see if William would arrive made her feel physically sick. Less than a week had passed since the point-to-point and it seemed to Christina like a year. She washed her hair in the scullery and Mary asked her if Mr. William was coming back.

"He's supposed to be coming to take me to the ball," Christina said, muffled. "But I don't think he will."

"William was always a boy for keeping his word." Mary said in her tart voice. But to Christina the words were like honey.

"Did your Aunt Grace send you a pretty dress this time? I took the box in—I guessed what it was."

"Oh, Mary, it's beautiful! You won't believe it. But—but suppose I get all dressed up, and he—he doesn't come?" Christina's voice quivered. She could cry at the thought of it, with her head under the achingly cold tap, hidden by her hair.

"If it's possible, he will come, Miss Christina. If not—well, that's life, dear."

Christina thought little of life, on Saturday. It rained, and every moment was an hour. Mary made her tea at five o'clock, and lit a fire in her bedroom. If she noticed the state Christina was in, she said nothing. At seven o'clock Christina started to get dressed. She was glad of the fire, because she could not

stop shivering. Or trembling. She did not know which. The
rain stopped, and a spring moon came out even before it was
dark, and a young vixen howled in the wild garden. Christina
slipped the dress over her head and it fell heavily down over
her petticoat. She eased the hips, and breathed in while Mary
did up the buttons down the back.

"Oh, Miss Christina, it's a treat! Fits you just right. As if
Miss Grace had made it on you!"

Christina sat down and Mary did her hair for her. It went
up at the back in a big coil, a more elegant coil than usual,
with one or two curls falling forward at the side of her neck in
a carefully casual manner. Mary was very good at hairdressing.

"I used to do Mrs. Russell's. Very particular she was. I
learned it all off her. Proper lady's maid I used to be in those
days. Before they spent all the money, that was. There used to
be five servants here then, Miss Christina. Easy days, they
were."

When she had finished, Christina looked quite beautiful,
even to her own eyes. She knew she had never looked like
this in her life before. Very smooth, very tidy, very cool, her
skin very white, her eyes very blue. But inside she felt dread-
fully sick, all nerved up for the disappointment. It was ten
minutes to eight.

"I don't think he's coming," she said.

"Here, I've put a handkerchief in your bag," Mary said,
brightly. "And there's your coat now. Pity it's not up to the
dress, but there, no one will see it in the dark. Now you wait
by the fire, dear, and I'll go down and be ready to let you
know as soon as he comes. If he can call without Mr. Russell
seeing him, I dare say it would be best. They can have their
argument when it's all over, tomorrow."

"If he comes," Christina said.

When Mary had gone, she stood in front of the fire, trying
to be calm and philosophical. But she kept shivering. "If he
comes up the drive," she thought, "I will see him from the
landing window." She opened the door quietly and went out
down the passage. The landing window looked out over the

front. The house was silent, and gloomy, only the branch of candles which Mary had left at the top of the stairs guttering dismally in the draughts. Christina looked out through the wet panes and saw only the empty paddocks, the weedy gravel, and the chestnuts tossing in a gusty breeze. "Nothing," she thought.

A door handle clicked behind her, and she turned around, startled. She had forgotten all about Mark, as if he did not exist any more. But, coming out of his room, he saw her standing by the window. He came to the top of the stairs and stood looking at her, without saying a word. He had his back to the light and she could not see his features, but she could sense his eyes raking over her, almost feel them, as she stared back at him. She tried to look as if nothing mattered, and whether she succeeded or not she could not guess. She only knew that a flame of humiliation seared her. She felt like a trodden black beetle. She lifted her chin and stared back. If she had turned away, she knew Mark would have laughed, and teased her, and she would not have survived that. But he did not even smile, and went on down the stairs and out of the front door.

Christina, about to dissolve into the dark agony of the greatest disappointment that she believed she would ever suffer in her life, looked out of the window, and saw Mark hesitate on the gravel. Setting off in the direction of the stables, he stopped and looked down the drive toward the road and, following his curiosity, Christina looked too and saw the shape of Mr. Dermot's Rolls-Royce nose into sight around the curve of the drive. It purred across the gravel like a great smooth cat, black flanks gleaming, headlights illuminating the whole façade of Flambards with a measured grandiloquent sweep like the loom of a lighthouse. It came to a halt outside the front door just as Mary came running up the stairs, her eyes sparkling with excitement and pleasure.

"Christina! Miss Christina! It's all right! He's here!"

Gone Away

It was as if the week had never happened. Mary helped her on with her coat, and she went downstairs and found William coming in at the front door, just the same as he had ever been.

"Oh, thank goodness you're ready," he said. "Let's go at once, before Father comes out to welcome me." He grinned at her, and held the door for her to slip through. Christina smiled at Mary, and hurried out to the car.

"There's a rug in the back. Can you get it? I'll stop at the gate and fix you up, but let's get clear first." William climbed into the driving seat. The engine was still running, and almost immediately the big car was sweeping around the drive once more, and heading for the road. William wore a cap with goggles pushed up, a heavy coat and a big woolen muffler. The dark firs spun past and the cold stung Christina's face. She shook out the tulle stole and wound it around her head to stop her elegant hair from being blown about.

"You're all right?" William asked.

"Oh, yes. Don't stop." Christina could not get away from Flambards fast enough. The big smooth motor excited her, with the lights sweeping the road ahead, the wind whistling around her ears.

"Where is it? Badstocks?"

"Yes." Christina hesitated. "I thought you weren't coming."

"But you got my note? I said I would." William sounded surprised.

"Oh, yes. But all the same, I wasn't sure. I didn't know what you were doing."

"This damned leg. I'm sorry." William changed gear badly, and the car jerked, meeting the hill. "I haven't driven the Rolls much. But Mr. Dermot said it was the only car to use for a ball." He laughed.

"But you haven't been at Mr. Dermot's all the week?"

"No, of course not. Only tonight, to change, and tell him what I was doing. I only got there at half-past six. I was in Farnborough this morning."

"What have you been doing? Have you got a job?"

"Oh, nothing definite yet. But lots of things to follow up. I think it will be all right. I know what I want, which is the main thing. I'm going to take my Aero Club ticket to convince them I can fly. And meanwhile, I've been promised a flight at Farnborough on Monday, and I've got an interview on Wednesday with Mr. O'Gorman—he's the head at Farnborough. You know there's going to be a Military Aeroplane Competition in the summer—that means the War Office wants to buy some planes, at last—so with things expanding like that, there should be room for me somewhere."

"With official people, War Office people—the Flying Corps, I mean—doesn't your leg matter?"

"It doesn't help," William said shortly.

To turn it into a joke, Christina said, "Mark said you wouldn't be able to dance. I told him you couldn't be worse than he was, and he wasn't very amused."

William laughed. "Good for you. And if I do tread on you, I reckon I'm a good deal lighter."

He slowed down for a carriage ahead. In the headlights Christina recognized Peter Lucas and his fiancée; she waved as they cautiously overtook them, but Peter had his hands too full with the frightened horse to reciprocate.

"It's time horses got educated," William complained.

"What's the use of a motor like this if you have to pass every horse at walking pace?"

Badstocks, set handsomely in its small home park on the top of a hill, backed with the big elms that had caused William such difficulty the week before, was a blaze of lights when they arrived. William parked the Rolls just outside the stable-yard, and left his cap and muffler on the seat. They walked around the tidy gravel together to the front door, and Christina saw William's doubtful glance toward the light and noise inside. He hesitated, fractionally, and then walked firmly forward, taking her arm very correctly for the steps; Christina felt that he had spurred himself mentally, facing a nasty jump. She could not understand why he wanted to take her, and the suspicion that it was merely to spite Mark returned, a cold drip on her happiness. She went through the door, chastened.

But it was impossible to stay downcast. Colonel and Mrs. Badstock and Mr. and Mrs. Lucas were waiting inside the door to welcome the guests, and William, far from being an outsider, was greeted with a heartiness that obviously disarmed him.

"Even if you are the first man to win our Open Race in an aeroplane," Lucas remarked, amid much laughter.

Christina went to take off her coat in the bedroom a maid showed her, and noticed the measuring-up glances of the other girls, through narrowed, cool eyes, at her dress. But her nervousness was steadied, not by confidence in her dress, but by the knowledge that she could ride better than the girls who watched her. She tidied her hair, changed her shoes and arranged the stole to hide a little of the bareness, then went back along the corridor to the top of the stairs.

This was the classic entrance of all the romantic novels she had read (borrowed from Mary), sweeping down the staircase to join the admiring beloved at the bottom. But William, although dutifully waiting, had his back to her, talking to Colonel Badstock, and did not see her till she had arrived at his elbow. He turned around, seeing the colonel smile at her, and Christina was gratified to see a genuine shock of surprise leap across his face.

"Why, Christina! Good God, I wouldn't have recognized you!"

"Oh, William, please, that's not the gracious way to put it," the colonel chided. He said to Christina, "He means it as a compliment, my dear, but these young men don't learn to phrase their appreciation as we did in my young day."

"It's absolutely ripping. Top hole, Christina old girl," William said, grinning.

"Oh, dear me!" The colonel rolled his eyes. "If you wish to savor a little real, old-world courtesy, Christina, please keep a dance for me later in the evening. I should be honored." He smiled, and turned around to greet some more arrivals.

William held his arm out for Christina and said, "Truly, Christina, you look lovely."

"Thank you," Christina said. Even if it was only to spite Mark, the evening was already the sweetest thing that had ever happened to her. She wanted to tell William that he looked lovely too, but she stood demurely while he gave their names to the footman to call out. She had never seen him in evening dress before either. She wondered where he had got it from. The high stiff collar, white tie, and black tails were immaculate.

The main feature of Badstocks was the old timber framed dining hall, which was always used for the ball. The original main part of the house, it now had other smaller and more convenient rooms opening off it, the rooms used by the family. Mrs. Badstock had log fires and lights everywhere, and in the main hall itself, there were log fires at each end, and a genuine minstrels gallery where now a six-piece dance band was playing "My Old Man Said Follow the Van." The atmosphere was cheerful and friendly, for everyone knew each other, although Christina took some time to recognize some of the elegant figures as the same she more commonly saw covered in mud and swearing dreadful oaths, perhaps stuck in a ditch, or pounding over sticky plow. Mark came in, alone, soon after their own arrival; he glowered at Christina, ignored William, and started talking to a smart blond girl in a very tight dress. Mark never had any trouble in attracting the girls' attention, Christina had discovered long ago.

"Doesn't Mark know us tonight then?" William asked, surprised.

"He hasn't spoken a word to me, since I told him I was coming here with you," Christina said.

"He was angry?"

"Yes."

"He doesn't own you, yet," William said, frowning. Christina hated the "yet." She looked up quickly at William, but he was watching Mark. "Who is the blond girl? A girl friend of his? She looks his sort."

"Amy Masters. She's hard on her horses." It was the only thing she knew about her, apart from her name.

William smiled. "I'm glad to hear some people are hard on their horses. I always thought it was invariably the other way around. It was with me."

Christina said, "*Emma Four's* hard on you. Far worse than a horse."

"*Emma Four* and I understand each other. I only hope this kite I'm going to fly on Monday is half as sweet-natured."

Christina had often been frightened for William's safety in the past, but not in the same way as his words now jerked her complacency. She felt quite suddenly as afraid for him as he must have felt himself the day Woodpigeon threw him at the ditch. The feeling was involuntary, and its violence shook her. She did not reply, not trusting her voice for a moment.

"Shall we try to dance?" William said cheerfully. "What is the music? Do you know? A waltz?"

"I think that's what the others are doing."

To her astonishment William, in spite of his leg, could dance quite well. Christina quickly forgot her qualms, her fears replaced by the present sweet reality of having his arms around her. After the past week's gloomy conjectures, she could scarcely believe it was happening, that she could possibly be so happy. "I can't imagine," she thought to herself, "being any happier than I am now, whatever is to happen." It was worth holding to, this feeling, while it existed. Such perfect happiness must by its nature be rare. She watched the room revolve over William's shoulder, absorbing the heady atmosphere, half seeing the passing faces which laughed and shone and spun. William's hand was warm and firm in hers.

Christina found, to her great surprise, that William was not the only person who wished to dance with her. As the champagne flowed and the music quickened, Christina was claimed time and time again by men whose horses she could picture even when she could not put a name to their faces. Flattered, and feeling that the night was not quite real, she danced continuously. William did not ask anyone else to dance, but found plenty of people to talk to—all men, Christina noted with satisfaction—when she was whirled away. Only Mark did not come near her, and when she passed him he did not smile. Christina noticed that he was drinking a good deal, but it did not show in his behavior.

Just before the supper interval, William came across to Christina firmly, and said, "This dance will be mine, Christina, else it wasn't worth coming."

He held her closely, and she put her cheek against his shoulder. "Just like Mary's novel," she thought. She was in a state of dreamlike bliss, which she knew had nothing to do with real life at all, yet she could give herself to it, and not worry. "Don't think," she said to herself. "Nothing good will come of thinking," and she remembered Aunt Grace's advice about drinking, and found herself replying, "This isn't the champagne. It's love." As the music finished, William said, "Look, I'll fetch something to eat and we'll take it out into the conservatory. It's too crowded in here."

The doors of the conservatory were open onto the garden, which looked over the valley. The rain had finished, and the fields dropped away beyond the clipped hedges to the distant swollen stream, picked out by a bright half-moon. The thorned sloe still gleamed white. The wet grass, hoof-churned, was a sea beneath the moon, smelling warm and pungent.

William came with some more champagne, and two platefuls of savory tidbits. They lodged the plates and glasses among the pots of camellia cuttings, and William said, "If anyone asks you to dance afterward, you can say you've promised them all to me."

A voice behind them said, "Except mine, of course, Christina. I insist."

Colonel Badstock put his plate down on an empty flowerpot and said to William, "Tell me about this strange animal you were riding last Saturday. I hear it's a brainchild of Dermot's down at Hanningford."

"Yes, sir. But don't judge her performance by last Saturday. She does stay up as a rule."

Christina, feeling she could afford to be magnanimous toward the interfering old colonel in the light of William's last remark to her, picked up her plate and started to eat. The colonel proved to be genuinely interested, and William became involved, but Christina was content. She crossed the tiled passage, and looked out over the moon-polished fields. The sky was clear, full of stars, framed by the camellias in their ornate china pots. The heady scent of the camellias was washed with the outside smell, honest and clean, that came through the open door, and Christina thought, "The camellia smell is tonight, but the other is everyday." It was gone at midnight, and the everyday would soon be back.

"Here, Christina, do you want a drink?"

Christina looked up in surprise, to see Mark standing beside her, holding out a glass of champagne.

"Oh!" She did not know what to say. She took the glass and put it on the bench, slightly suspicious. Mark appeared to be still sober, so she did not know what explained his change of heart.

"I haven't had a chance to speak to you," he said. "You've been too much in demand."

"As you haven't spoken to me for the last five days, I didn't really expect you to bother tonight." Christina said discouragingly.

Mark, surprisingly, looked almost sheepish. "Well, I was annoyed. I'm sorry." He paused. "I wanted you to come with me."

Christina looked at Mark nervously. He spoke with none of his usual airiness. His voice was slightly thick with drink, but his eyes were steady and serious. She glanced behind but William had disappeared, having been taken off by the colonel to meet another flying man.

"I didn't enjoy it with you very much last year," she said, still hoping to discourage Mark. "If you remember, you were too drunk to take me home. Peter Lucas took me in his carriage."

"Yes. I don't remember, to tell you the truth, so you must be right. I'm sorry, Christina. I—I suppose I drink too much."

"Yes," Christina said. This contrite Mark was a complete mystery to her, and she began to suspect that he was as drunk as he had been last year, but with a different effect. Yet his gaze was quite steady, slightly unnerving in its sincerity. The familiar features, still so like and yet unlike William's in the way that had baffled her when she had first come to Flambards, were still compelling, in spite of their scars. She knew him well; they had been through most extremes together out hunting, from roaring exhilaration to cold, boring frustration, and they had spent many hours to and from meets in moods that had ranged from pleasant accord to bitter animosity. She had no reason, she thought, to feel that he was a stranger now. But, warily, she turned her head away and looked down across the fields. There were people coming and going behind them in the conservatory, chatting and laughing, and a man was demonstrating a golf stroke on the terrace outside, very much in earnest. The band was playing some interval music that Christina overheard someone say was by Mr. Elgar. It struck her as a remarkably bizarre choice, and yet the chords, even as performed by a swing sextet, had a strange and stirring relevance just at that moment, full of a beauty that she could not understand, full of the doubts and uncertainties she knew so well, and suggesting a sadness that she was sure was very close to her present happiness. She kept her gaze on the fields outside, not saying anything.

"Do you like that music?" Mark asked.

"Yes."

"It makes me think of what is going to happen," Mark said, very obscurely.

"What do you mean?"

"Don't you ever think about the future?"

"Of course. Surely everybody does?"

"Yes, well, that's what I mean. I don't think there is going to be much of a future, and when I think about it, I can get ruddy miserable, like that music."

Mark was assuredly drunk. But Christina had an instinct that he might touch something, however obscure, through his drink, that he would not dare to think about in sobriety. He was deadly serious.

"What do you mean?" she asked.

"Oh, that there's not much time, I suppose. And we ought to stop and think sometimes, about all this—" he nodded across the moonlit fields—"and about what matters."

"Why isn't there much time?"

"If there's a war, I mean. We take all this for granted—hunting and all that—and then when the war comes . . ."

"What war?"

"It is too good to last. Soon there will be a war. But I don't mind, really, if there is. As long as you know what you are fighting for, you can go and do your whack—you might even enjoy it. And I would fight for all this." He gestured out across the fields again. Christina did not move, feeling cold and rather frightened. Mark straightened up, frowning. He picked one of the camellia flowers, and twisted it around his fingers.

"I'm making such a fool of myself, but I have got feelings, Christina. I would go out and get killed, willingly, if I thought all this would never change. The old places, like this, and Flambards too, and the old way of life. This countryside—there's nowhere else in the world like England. You can keep your progress—Will's aeroplanes, for example. What good is all that rubbish? He will get killed, for no reason at all, and everything that is good and real is right under his nose all the time. The scientists are rushing headlong to destroy us all, and they do not see that the old ways are best. They have endured for centuries, and will go on long after the machines have fallen to pieces, and the scientists have killed us all with their cleverness."

He stopped, frowning again, bewildered at his own excess of words.

"I expect you think I am a fool," he added, with unwonted humility.

"No," Christina said. She was touched by Mark's speech, even with all its flagrant paradoxes staring her in the face. She wanted to say, violently, "What about Dick? What about Violet? Would they feel the same about your old ways?" But she said nothing.

"You know what I'm rambling on about, Christina, don't you?" Mark said. "What I'm getting at? When I say there's not much time, I just thought—if you want Flambards—we could get married fairly soon. Before hunting starts again."

"Mark!" Christina knocked over her glass in her start of surprise, and it broke on the tiles. She turned around and stared at him, incredulously.

"You—are you proposing? Are you asking me to marry you?"

"Yes."

"But—but I've never led you to suppose that I—I—." Christina was at a loss for words, taken completely by surprise. She was aghast at the turn the conversation had taken.

"It just seems the obvious thing, surely?" Mark said. "If you want to stay at Flambards. You don't want to be just the housekeeper do you, like Mary?" There was a touch of asperity, the old Mark whom Christina recognized.

"But you don't marry someone because it's the obvious thing," Christina said. "There's more to it than that! You haven't just supposed I was going to marry you, after all this time, the same as you supposed I was going to come to this ball with you?" Her dismay was turning to indignation, and Mark glowered at her in the way she knew so well. They were back on familiar ground again.

"Look, I may not have chosen the right words, but do you want me to go down on one knee or something? I haven't supposed anything. I just suggested we could get married. I thought you would think it a good idea."

Christina said, "Well, I don't. I'm sorry, Mark," she added, trying hard to be gracious. "But I—I—oh, it's no good! I can't say I will think about it, because I won't. We don't think the same way. We would never get on. I should hate you to feel that I will come around to seeing it differently, because I shan't."

Mark looked at her closely, angrily. "There's nothing between you and Will, is there?"

Christina flared up. "How can there be? He's going away, isn't he? British Columbia, if your father has his way."

Mark was frighteningly like his father. She had always known it, but now as he came up close to her, his dark eyebrows drawn angrily together, she almost felt that it was the bullying old man himself.

"If I thought you and Will were up to anything, I'd send him farther than British Columbia, believe me!"

"You don't own us!" Christina hissed at him. "We're not your servants!"

She pushed past him. He tried to hold her, putting his hand on her arm, but she snatched herself away and ran out of the conservatory and back into the big hall, where the band was beginning to play dance music again. She had had many fierce rows with Mark before, but this was one that she did not think he would forgive. She looked anxiously for William, her evening shattered. The dancers whooped past her, all very merry now, and she had to edge her way through.

Suddenly William was at her side.

"Christina, I'm sorry! I was just coming to look for you. What's the matter? Is something wrong?"

"Will! Oh, please—"

"What is it? Here—" They had to step back, jostled by the big circle of dancers doing the grand chain of the Lancers. "Let's find somewhere out of the way." He grasped her hand and eased her through the crowd. They escaped from the hall,

and found a small library where a fire burned, and a black re-
triever slumbered in a homely way on the hearth rug.

"Now tell me," William said. "Is it Mark?"

"He asked me to marry him."

"Do you want to?"

"No. Never. I shall never marry him."

"You told him that?"

"Yes. He was very angry. He was just like Russell. He—he
said there isn't much time. He said there is going to be a war."

William was staring into the fire. He pushed one of the
logs with his stiff leg.

"Is there going to be a war?" Christina asked.

"Most people say not, but I think it's very likely. That's why
I'm so keen to get into Farnborough. There will be so much
to do."

His gravity impressed Christina. She was conscious of the
cold fear that Mark had touched off in her taking hold again,
very solid and real this time.

"If there's a war, you would go on flying? Or would you
fight?"

"I think it would be a matter of flying and fighting, Christina. I think of a war in terms of the aeroplane, just as Mark
—no doubt—sees himself galloping into battle with the cavalry."
He looked up, and smiled apologetically. "But it won't be tomorrow. What are you going to do, that's more to the point?
Did Mark make you an ultimatum? Is living at Flambards
conditional on your marrying him?"

"I don't know." She remembered the expression on Mark's
face. "I think, if I don't marry him, I shall have to go away. It
will be very awkward if I don't." To herself she also thought it
would be very awkward if she did. Her future security, within
a space of ten minutes, had been blasted by Mark's proposal.
And yet, strangely, the idea of a future without a home meant
far less to her at that moment than the prospect of a future
without William. It was very difficult to stand before him,
sensible and calm, when with every instinct she wanted to
fling herself on his white starched breast and say, "I don't

care where I am, as long as I'm with you." Just like a music-hall song, she thought. It was a terrible effort, turning it into a joke, almost beyond her powers. Her throat tightened ominously.

William said, "As my father remarked when that animal crippled me, that makes two of us."

"What do you mean?"

"Two of us thrown out of Flambards. If you've no plans, Christina, perhaps we could work something out together."

She looked at him blankly. He looked remarkably cheerful. "It's all right, Christina," he said gently. "Don't look as if it matters so."

"It's you that matters," she said numbly.

He said, "You wouldn't be afraid, would you? There's something in what Mark says, you know—if there's not much time we shouldn't be wasting it. You wouldn't be afraid to come away?"

"With you?"

"Yes." He smiled again. "I'm not making an improper proposal. I can't offer you anything at all for a year or two, but if, perhaps, you were to go to your Aunt Grace's, you could decide what you want, away from Flambards. And when I have got a job, and earned some money and have some sort of a future, I will come and propose to you, very properly. Do you think that's a good idea?"

"Yes," Christina whispered,

"You might accept, do you think?"

"Oh, yes. I will."

"You must think of all the drawbacks," he said softly. "Aunt Grace will point them all out to you. You must listen."

"Yes, I will."

"And it's not for your money, you know that? You can give it all away, every penny. It would make no difference."

"Yes. No, I mean."

"Shall we go now?"

"Now?" Christina's eyes opened very wide.

"We could be at Aunt Grace's by morning. Mr. Dermot said

I could use the motor as I pleased until I went back to Farnborough."

"Very well." Christina could hear her heart thumping.

"Go and get your coat. I shall wait for you by the door."

Christina went out of the room, across the hall and slowly up the carpeted stairs to the candle-lit bedroom. People passed her laughing; some girls chattered in front of the mirrors, but she saw nobody. She pulled her old black astrakhan coat over the lovely dress: the eloping dress, she thought, with a pang of compunction. She felt calm, and very sure that she was doing the right thing. But she also knew, with unwavering certainty, that what she was choosing to do meant giving up the self-sufficiency she had spent so many stubborn years acquiring. If she loved William, she would become infinitely vulnerable. She knew him well enough to realize that the greatest part of his love was reserved for *Emma Four* and her kind and, however tenderly he might cherish a wife, the wife would never come first. To love William demanded that she would have to encourage him in the very thing that, in her heart, she knew was likely to rob her of him altogether.

The other girls had gone. Christina pushed back the closed curtains and looked out of the window.

"If you are afraid," she said to herself (and she knew that this fear was what William had meant when he had asked her if she was afraid), "there is always Flambards. It's not too late." But the unchanging peace of Flambards seemed beside William's offer the unchanging peace of a tomb. "No going back," Christina told herself sternly. "There will be nowhere to go back to." She let the curtains drop again and went out of the room.

This time, coming down the stairs had all the significance in the world. There was no one to see her, only William waiting, one hand on the newel post. He looked rather anxious. Christina felt deeply content.

"You're sure?" he said. "I want you, Christina. But it won't be easy for you. You must make sure you listen to Aunt Grace." He took her hand and led her to the front door. "I forgot to tell you—"

"What?"

"I love you terribly. All this last week . . . I don't want to make you unhappy, and I shall because of flying. I shouldn't ask you. Aunt Grace will tell you all this."

"Yes," said Christina firmly. "I know all that. I have thought. But it doesn't matter." She felt quite sure: secure enough to laugh now. "It's you who are afraid!"

"Only of running out of gas before we get to London," William said, smiling suddenly.

The doubts were gone. They walked down the gravel path to where the big Rolls was parked just outside the stableyard.

"I am sorry for Mark!" William whispered.

"I thought you asked me to the ball to spite him," Christina said. "I was sure of it. I didn't think you would come."

"When I asked you, a year ago, it was to tease Mark, it's true. But last week, when I knew I was going away, I couldn't bear to think of his taking you. I didn't want him to—to touch you. Nothing would have stopped me from coming tonight."

He opened the door of the Rolls and held it while Christina slid into the leather seat. He pulled the rug out of the back, and tucked it around her. The air was cold and damp, smelling of rain, the stars coming and going.

"It will be a long ride."

"It's a splendid horse."

"It has brakes," William said. "All horses should have brakes." He gave her his woolen muffler, pulled on his cap and went around to the front to start the engine. It broke into a soft, powerful rhythm. Christina felt her inside contract with excitement and joy. She tried to remember that it would be hard, that she would be hurt and afraid, that there was going to be a war, but she just wanted to laugh. "I am strong enough," she thought. William was lighting the headlights, impatient, half frowning. She watched his face, the dark eyes lit by the flaring carbide. At the same moment she heard the scrunch of hoofs on the gravel and Mark's voice, sharp and suspicious, "Are you taking Christina back to Flambards?"

She turned around and saw the white shape of Woodpigeon in the darkness, Mark holding him in with his heavy hands, so that he tucked his nose in, easing his jaw for the pain. In that moment, strangely, it was the horse Christina felt for: kindly, mellowed Woodpigeon, whom she would never ride again. William straightened up and came to the car door, ducking warily under Woodpiegon's head. He paused, and looked up at Mark, very cool.

"I'm taking her away," he said, and turned and got awkwardly into the car, easing off the brake immediately.

If Mark had had a whip, Christina thought he would have used it, as he once had used it on Dick. But he could only shout, above the revving up of the engine, and his words, slurred with drink, were impossible to catch. Woodpigeon, sensing his temper, half-reared, flinging himself away from the moving car, but Mark in his rage spurred him furiously around again. As William changed gear and the Rolls gathered speed, Mark put Woodpigeon into a canter. They went through the gates of Badstocks side by side, the big white horse lengthening his stride. Christina could see Mark's face, and his lips shouting. The car lights swept across the road, and William put his foot down on the accelerator. He turned to Christina, and she saw that he was laughing.

"That horse!" he shouted. "He still terrifies me!"

Woodpigeon was galloping, his hoofs flinging sparks, but gradually the powerful car roared ahead. Christina felt the wind catch her scarf, and her smooth hair start to fly out. Mark's words were whirled away. The night air buffeted her, stabbing with cold fingers. William pulled down his goggles, and reached for her with his left arm, watching the narrow road.

"You're not afraid?" he shouted.

"No!"

It has started, she thought. She was afraid, and magnificently happy altogether. She pressed close to William, and watched the car lights veer down the long valley, splintering the dark of her familiar fields.

ABOUT THE AUTHOR

K. M. Peyton is the well-known author of many distinguished books for young people, including the critically acclaimed Flambards trilogy and its sequel, *Flambards Divided*. Born in Birmingham, England, Ms. Peyton spent four years as a student at the Manchester School of Art. She is married to an artist and they live with their two daughters in Essex, England. When she is not out riding or sailing with her family or writing a book, Ms. Peyton likes to go for long walks, listen to music, read history, or do gardening. Her most recently published novels include *Dear Fred*, a young adult novel about horse racing, and *Going Home*, an adventure story for younger readers.

ABOUT THE ARTIST

Victor G. Ambrus, known for his spirited drawings, has illustrated many books for young people. He has also written several children's books, and has won many awards for his work as an author and illustrator. Mr. Ambrus was runner-up for the Kate Greenaway Medal in 1964 and 1965, and winner of the 1964 Carnegie Medal. Born in Budapest, Hungary, Mr. Ambrus studied at the Academy of Fine Arts there. He and his wife, who is also an artist, live with their son in Hampshire, England.